THE INCREDIBLE COUSINS

and

The Magic Caboose

Written by

M. E. GERHARDT

As told to him by:

HENRY GALLAGHER

WESTON GALLAGHER

CHARLOTTE WISMER

ANNABELLE RINDA

QUINN GALLAGHER

GARRETT WISMER

Copyright 2017 by M. E. Gerhardt

Incredible Cousins PUBLISHING

First edition: 2017

10 9 8 7 6 5 4 3 2 1

ISBN: 13: 978-19757253334

ISBN: 10: 1975725336

Cover art by Renate Harshaw

Cover design by Heil Design

Editing by Annabelle Rinda

Back page photograph by Heather Gallagher

Visit us at: www.incrediblecousins.com

FORWARD

I had the great joy of having three wonderful daughters who have provided me with six terrific grandchildren, all of them living nearby. For Christmas last year I decided to give the grandchildren a special present. I told them I would write a book, and the six of them would be the main characters. I also told them they would participate in building the story, inviting them to select their character names, their specific superpower, and asking them to suggest mysteries the club could solve. I believe our regular creative meetings and interactions stimulated their creativity and brought the cousins closer to each other. It was an exercise that delivered benefits on several levels, and I thank all six grandchildren for their input and support.

CHAPTER ONE

It was like Christmas in August. Annabelle Ronda lived with her parents in a cozy cottage on a horse farm, where Annabelle's mom managed the barn and gave riding lessons. Every year the family celebrated Annabelle's birthday at the swimming pool that sat right next to their cottage. This year, Annabelle's mom had invited her two sisters to bring their kids early for a special treat. She was taking them all on a trail ride in the woods.

The six cousins were excited. They helped tack up their horses and then mounted them and followed Annabelle's mom out of the barn and onto the path. Annabelle, age twelve today, rode her pony, Cody behind her mom, who was riding Beau. Next in the line were two of the Gallahan brothers, Chugga, also age twelve, riding Moonlight, a silver mare, and his younger brother Quinn, age ten, riding Flame, a chestnut gelding.

Fourth in line came the two Wise kids, Charlotte, age twelve on Ace, a black gelding with a white mane and her little brother Garrett, age six, riding Sugar, a small white mare. Bringing up the rear, where he could keep an eye on things, was Henry, the oldest Gallahan brother at fourteen, riding Rocky, a chocolate colored gelding.

As the group rode along over fields and pastures, they gradually grew comfortable with their horses. Henry and Annabelle had ridden for years, but it was the first time for the rest of the group. After a half hour of riding, Annabelle's mom's phone suddenly rang. She answered and listened, then said "OK" and cut the connection. She stopped and the entire line stopped behind her. She turned to Annabelle.

"That was Dad," she said. "There is someone who wants to board a horse here, a very famous one. We have to go back so I can talk to them."

The cousins groaned as a group.

"Can't we ride a little longer?" begged Annabelle. "It's my birthday. Please!"

Her mom looked back down the trail toward the barn, considering. Everyone seemed comfortable, but still.

"Garrett, will you be OK if I go back and you ride along with the others?"

Everyone turned to look at Garrett. His answer would decide the fate of the ride.

"Sure!" he said, and everyone secretly cheered.

"OK. Annabelle, you can lead for anther fifteen minutes, but then you have to come back. Your other guests will be coming soon."

There was a cheer from the group. Annabelle's mom eyed them all, one at a time.

"Stay in the line and stay safe." She looked at Annabelle. "And don't go onto the new property Mister Layman just bought. We haven't ridden there yet."

They all agreed and watched her ride off toward the barn. When they were sure she was actually going to let them ride alone, there was another cheer.

"Awesome," said Chugga.

"Let's go!" shouted Quinn. Annabelle turned toward the two brothers.

"Stay with me or we'll get into trouble, OK?" Annabelle and looked back at Garrett. "Are you OK, Garrett?"

Garrett nodded and Annabelle led them off, riding further away from the barn. Everyone stayed in line and all went well until they reached the edge of the property where Annabelle's mom had told her to turn around. She stopped and they all looked out at the open fields in front of them, and the green woods to the right.

"This is where we turn around," Annabelle said as she pulled Cody to the right and started back the way they came. Everyone followed her, but suddenly, Henry called out.

"Hey, wait a second."

Annabelle stopped the line and looked back at Henry.

"What's the matter?"

Henry was fighting his horse, trying to keep it headed in the right direction.

"This stupid horse won't turn around. He wants to go the other way."

Annabelle sighed and turned Cody around. She rode back to Henry, who was clearly struggling with his horse. Annabelle stopped Cody next to the horse and scolded him.

"Rocky, what are you doing? It's time to go home."

The gelding turned an eye toward Annabelle, shook his head and snorted. He turned away and started toward the woods. Henry kept pulling on the reins, but to no avail.

Rocky was determined. Suddenly all of the other horses started following him, ignoring the pleading of their riders. Annabelle continued to shout, but there was no stopping them.

Everyone just held on as best they could as the horses began trotting into the woods. Suddenly they came to a clearing and they all stopped, pawing the ground, clearly nervous. The cousins just stared. Sitting in the middle of the clearing was an old, dilapidated, run down wreck of a structure.

"What the heck is that?" Asked Chugga.

"Looks like a caboose," offered Henry.

"A what?" asked Garrett.

"A caboose. It's the last car on a train," answered Henry.

"What's it doing here?" Asked Charlotte. "There's no train tracks anywhere."

"What a dump," said Quinn.

Annabelle watched the horses as they nervously pawed the ground. They had been drawn here, she thought, but they also seem uncomfortable. She wished she could talk to them.

"I don't like it here," said Garrett, a little scared by the building. "Can we go now?"

"No! Let's check it out." Called Quinn as he struggled down from his horse.

"I don't think we should. It's not our property." Annabelle warned.

"Technically, it is," Henry argued. "Your mom said Mister Layman just bought the property. And, you're allowed to ride anywhere on his property, right?"

Annabelle shrugged. She supposed he was right, but her mom had told her not to go onto the new property.

"We should go back," she said, but she didn't really mean it. There was something about the old caboose that was holding her there. She watched Quinn as he walked toward the building. Suddenly Henry called out.

"Hold on a second, Quinn."

Quinn stopped and looked back at Henry, who turned and looked at Charlotte. Both Charlotte and her little brother Garrett had visual problems from birth, and both wore glasses. But Henry had observed over the years that while Charlotte might not see all that well with her eyes, she saw exceptionally well with her heart. He felt that they needed that skill now.

"Charlotte, what do you think? Is it OK?" Henry asked and pointed toward the caboose with his chin. "The caboose. Is it safe?"

Charlotte turned her body and peered at the sad structure huddled in the clearing. Quinn was right, it definitely was a wreck. She could make out that it had once been a caboose, the last car on a train. But those days had been gone for years. It certainly hadn't been painted this century, and the weather over the years had rotted most of the wood.

The front door and the side door were both hanging from their hinges, and the windows in the small area built out on top of the roof were all broken. The words UNION

PACIFIC were stenciled on the front in faded white paint. She took a deep breath and tried to get a sense of the place. After a moment, she turned to Henry.

"Well, I agree with Quinn, the outside is a disaster. And I have no idea how it got here. But, I think it's OK. In fact, I feel like it is something quite special."

Henry nodded and turned back to Quinn.

"OK. Check it out."

Quinn nodded and turned back to face the caboose. They all watched as he walked toward it. The wheels were gone and it sat on the ground, a little lopsided, a little sad looking. Quinn stopped a few feet from the main door. Oddly enough, there was a large flat rock right in front of the elevated door that allowed him to step right up to the level of the door. When he stepped on the rock, the door smoothly swung open on its own, and Quinn had to jump back to get out of the way. He turned and looked at his big brother, hoping he had an explanation for what had just happened.

Henry just stared at the door and everyone else just sat, trying to decide what they should do next. Suddenly Annabelle's phone broke the silence, and they all jumped at the sound. It was Annabelle's father. She answered, listened and said "OK, dad." And hung up. She took up Cody's reigns.

"We have to go, right now. The guests are arriving."

"OK," Henry replied. "But, we're coming back here tomorrow."

"Definitely," added Chugga.

10

They all turned their suddenly compliant horses away from the caboose, and they all glanced back several times as they rode away from the strange building that sat in the clearing.

CHAPTER TWO

All six cousins were in the barn the next day by ten o'clock in the morning. It had not been easy, but their persistence paid off, and, one by one their parents had caved in and delivered them to the barn. However, they had not been able to convince Annabelle's mom to let them ride, so they were going to have to walk to the woods.

"Well, we might as well get going," Henry said and stood. He was over six feet tall, and very thin, a combination that brought more than a few cheap shots from his classmates. Annabelle and Charlotte were with him in the barn, talking to the horses as they stroked their sides. Both girls had long hair, and both wore glasses. They stopped and turned toward Henry.

"OK," Annabelle said. She looked around and asked Charlotte. "Where is Garrett?"

"I'm over here," Garrett called from the next row of stalls. Charlotte walked around the corner to find him standing in front of Sugar, the white mare he had ridden the day before.

"Hey, buddy," she said, and he glanced up at her.

"She's really pretty," he said as he patted the nose of the horse.

"Yeah, she is. Time to go. OK?"

Garrett stared at the horse for a few more seconds, then waved to it.

"See ya, Sugar!"

They all walked outside to find Chugga and Quinn flipping water bottles in the air. The group started out toward the rear of the property and Chugga and Quinn followed. They were a hundred yards up the slope when Annabelle's mother called out to them.

"Be back by eleven thirty."

Annabelle turned and waved, and set her phone alarm for 11:15. They resumed walking and were soon out of sight of the barn. They chatted quietly among themselves, each carrying their own expectations of what they would find in the clearing today.

They entered the woods but it seemed denser than before. And yesterday there was a sort of glow in the sky that helped guide them, but today it was not there. Nevertheless, within ten minutes they found the clearing.

They all stopped and stood staring at the dilapidated train car. It certainly hadn't gotten any nicer looking since they had seen it last. Finally Chugga spoke.

"Uh, does anybody see anything a little strange about this thing?"

They all concentrated a little harder, trying to find something stranger than normal on this already strange structure. Chugga gave them a few seconds, then answered his own question.

"It's August, right?"

"Yeah," Henry agreed. "It's hot already, and it's not even noon yet. So?"

"So, what's snow doing around the base of this thing?"

Everyone turned their attention to the spot where the caboose base met the ground. Sure enough, there was snow clinging to the bottom of the caboose.

"I find this somewhat disturbing," offered Annabelle.

Quinn broke ranks and stepped toward the caboose. He walked right up to it and knelt down. He reached out and scooped up a handful of snow.

"It is snow!" he announced, and the rest of the group hurried up and began grabbing hands full of the cold, white powder. Quinn fashioned a snowball and tossed it at Henry, hitting him on the shoulder.

"Cut it out, Quinn," Henry shouted. Just then the door to the caboose opened and the group jumped back. They looked at the door and at each other, wondering who would be the first to take some action. Henry was the closest to the door, and he was, after all, the oldest. He took a deep breath and stepped toward the open door.

He paused at the threshold, took another deep breath and then took a step up and peered inside. The space was completely empty. He turned back to the group.

"It's OK. It's empty. Just a bunch a cob webs and a lot of animal poop" he assured them all.

"Animal droppings," Annabelle corrected.

"Right." Henry said. He turned back and stepped inside. He took a sharp breath and stopped cold. The space was suddenly spotless and completely decorated. "What the heck?" Henry said out loud.

"What's the matter?" Charlotte asked.

Henry just stood and stared, so the rest of the group piled inside past him.

"Real funny, Henry" Quinn said as he looked around at the beautifully decorated space.

"Awesome," Chugga said and walked around the group and headed directly for the dining table, which was covered with every kind of food one could imagine. The rest of the group followed him and they spent the next five minutes sampling the array of tasty dishes. Finally, Garrett asked the question they were all thinking.

"Who made all of this food?"

Quinn answered. "I don't know, but it's really good. It's like being in a clubhouse."

Henry moved away from the table and walked around the room. He was surprised at how bright the space was. He stopped and moved a print covered curtain aside and looked out one of the many windows.

"Hey," came Charlotte's voice over his shoulder. He glanced at Charlotte.

"Hey," he replied.

"So, where did all of these windows come from?" Charlotte asked. "There were, like no windows on the outside at this level."

Henry shook his head.

"I don't know."

Chugga walked up and stood next to Henry.

"Weird place, huh?"

"I know, right?" Charlotte answered.

She turned around to look for Garrett and saw him sitting on an oriental rug playing with Star Wars figurines she hadn't noticed before. She saw Annabelle peering intently out one of the windows on the back of the caboose.

What are you looking at, girl friend? Charlotte thought to herself. Annabelle turned her head, ready to reply, and was surprised that Charlotte wasn't there. She turned further around and found Charlotte across the room.

"Did you just ask me a question?" Annabelle asked.

"Uh, no," Charlotte stammered, embarrassed.

"Huh," Annabelle said.

"What did you think I said?" Charlotte asked, her curiosity getting to her.

"It sounded like you asked me what I was looking at."

Charlotte took a sharp breath. *"This is too weird,"* she thought to herself.

"What's too weird?' Annabelle responded.

Charlotte stared at Annabelle and decided to try an experiment.

"I think I can communicate with you by telepathy," she thought in her head, aiming the thought toward Annabelle. Annabelle jumped back as if pushed. She stared at Charlotte, trying to make sense of what was happening. She took a few breaths to calm herself, and nodded. She

had definitely heard Charlotte, loud and clear inside her head. And she had definitely not seen Charlotte's lips move.

She focused on Charlotte, who was waiting for a reaction.

"I heard you. Can you hear me?" Annabelle thought back.

"Oh, my, God," replied Charlotte.

They both suddenly looked around at the other kids, but it didn't seem like anyone else had heard.

"Maybe they can only hear if we focus on them," Annabelle thought, shrugging.

"Try it," Charlotte responded.

Annabelle nodded and focused on Henry, who had his back to her.

"Henry, what are you looking at?"

Henry shrugged and turned around looking for Annabelle.

"Nothing. Just looking to see what's out there," Henry said out loud. Annabelle turned to Charlotte.

"This is very weird," Annabelle thought.

"Tell me about it." Charlotte replied.

They rounded up the rest of the group and gradually discovered that they could all speak to each other through mental telepathy.

Quinn particularly liked it.

"This is like having a super power," he thought, and they all agreed.

They were all trying out their new skills when Annabelle's phone alarm buzzed.

"We've got to go!" she said in a loud voice. Everyone groaned, but knew they'd best be going. They certainly didn't want to be told they could not come back to the caboose again. They tumbled out of the building and started across the clearing. Annabelle looked back and noticed the door was still open.

"Better close the door," she thought to Henry. He nodded and turned around. He stepped up the one step and reached in for the door handle. As he pulled the door shut, he happened to glance inside. The space was empty, only dirt, cobwebs and animal poop on the floor.

"Droppings", Henry thought to himself and smiled, shaking his head.

CHAPTER THREE

Everyone was excited about what had happened, so Henry decided not to mention what he had seen when he went back to close the door. Instead he tried to join the conversation. Garrett was talking.

"That was so cool. I want to go back there again. When can we go back again?"

Henry noted that Garrett had spoken the words aloud. He was probably having trouble grasping the concept of teleconnecting. Charlotte spoke next, also out loud.

"I wonder if we will be able to connect with our friends. That would be so cool."

"Or our parents." Annabelle added.

"Not so cool," injected Chugga.

"Can we do that mind thing out here, or just in the clubhouse?" asked Quinn.

"Let's try and see," suggested Charlotte. She looked at Chugga and thought.

"Was the food good?"

Chugga smiled and nodded.

"Yep."

"Awesome," replied Charlotte.

Henry chimed in.

"I like what Quinn called the place. Let's call it our clubhouse, OK?"

Everyone nodded in agreement and kept walking. Before they knew it, they were back at the barn and found all of their parents there chatting.

"We'd better not say anything to anyone about the clubhouse, or this teleconnecting thing," Henry cautioned the group.

"Why not?" asked Quinn, disappointed. He wanted to show off to everyone.

"Nobody will believe us, for one thing," Annabelle offered.

"I'm not sure I believe it," Chugga chimed in.

"But we could show them," argued Quinn.

His mom called out to him as they approached.

"Hey, Quinn. Did you guys have fun?"

"Yeah. It was great," he called back.

"Can we come back tomorrow?" he asked.

Several parents chimed in at once, voicing several reasons why that would not be possible.

"But mom!" he started to complain.

"Cool it!" Henry thought, trying to calm him. *"Don't get too excited about it. They'll wonder what we're up to."*

Quinn got it and nodded.

"OK, mom."

"Hey, Annabelle," Charlotte thought. *"Try to contact me tonight. Let's see how far away this teleconnecting thing works."*

"OK," Annabelle replied.

They all said their goodbyes to each other, silently agreeing to stay in touch via their new 'super power'. It was going to be a very interesting night.

CHAPTER FOUR

None of the cousins could wait to try out their new power. As soon as they could get a few minutes away from the adults, they closed themselves in their rooms and started thinking. First they tried to contact their parents, and were actually relieved to find out that their parents didn't have the power. They also tried to reach a few friends without any luck. They then turned their attention to their cousins.

Henry easily contacted Charlotte, even though she lived miles away. After confirming with her that she also could not contact her parents, he told her about the clubhouse turning back into an empty space when they left. Charlotte connected with Annabelle to fill her in on what Henry had told her, and Quinn, Chugga and Garrett connected with each other and discussed soccer, lacrosse and the cool things they had seen and eaten in the clubhouse.

The next day, Annabelle's best friend, Stella came over and they were allowed to saddle up two horses and ride out to the woods. Stella was on Beau and Annabelle was on Cody. Annabelle was very excited about showing Stella the clubhouse. She was hoping that getting Stella inside would be all it would take to allow her to teleconnect with Stella. After all, they were best friends. The closer they got to the clearing, the more she could feel Cody's reaction, a mixture of anticipation and concern.

Annabelle's anticipation also grew as they approached, and when they finally entered the clearing Annabelle stopped Cody. Stella stopped next to her and they sat quietly for a moment, Stella looking around and Annabelle staring at the clubhouse. Most of the snow seemed to be gone, but other than that, there was no visible change to the run down structure. She wondered what Stella was thinking, and finally couldn't wait any longer.

"So, what do you think?" Annabelle asked.

"About what?" replied Stella, peering at Annabelle.

Annabelle gestured toward the clubhouse.

"This."

Stella looked around and shrugged.

"It's nice."

"Nice?" Annabelle replied, somewhat disappointed. She certainly wouldn't have used the word 'nice' to describe the clubhouse. Shabby, run down, weird, out of place, unbelievable maybe, but not nice.

Stella nodded.

"Yes. It's a nice, quiet little clearing." Stella was struggling to come up with a good description, since her friend obviously liked the small open space in the woods.

"I like how the sun shines through the trees," she tried. "It makes nice patterns on the grass. And the yellow flowers are very nice."

Annabelle was getting frustrated.

"What about the caboose?" she almost shouted in frustration.

Stella looked around the space again and then turned to Annabelle.

"What caboose?"

Annabelle was stunned. She peered closely at Stella, tying to see if she was teasing her. When she decided that Stella was not putting her on, she took a deep breath. She really couldn't see the caboose! As they sat there, a small deer appeared on the far side of the clearing, stared at them for a moment, and then ran behind the caboose into the woods.

"Wow," said Stella, instantly forgetting Annabelle's question about the caboose. "Let's follow her," Stella said and urged her pony forward. Annabelle almost called out a warning as Stella rode directly for the caboose, but what happened next left her speechless. At first Beau hesitated when he got near the caboose, but Stella urged him forward and they rode straight through the caboose and into the woods on the far side of the clearing.

Annabelle was stunned. Stella had ridden right through the caboose as if it wasn't even there. After a moment Annabelle recovered and gently urged Cody forward.

When she reached the clubhouse she stopped Cody and leaned forward. She reached her hand out and touched the solid wall of the caboose. She could clearly not ride through the caboose like Stella had. She was trying to figure out this new piece of information when Stella called from the woods.

"Annabelle, hurry!"

Annabelle sat still, very confused. What was going on here? Finally Cody shook and snorted, rousing her.

"OK. Let's go."

She tugged on the reins and pointed Cody around the caboose and into the woods, more confused than ever.

CHAPTER FIVE

That night Annabelle teleconnected with the whole group, telling them about the incident with Stella. At first no one believed her, but eventually they all came around to believing that anything was possible with their new clubhouse. Henry was riding the next day in a horse show at a riding stable near Annabelle's house, and they all agreed to try to get their parents to bring them, and then lobby for a stop at Annabelle's afterwards.

They were all successful, and the group watched Henry take a first and a third in two competitions before all three families retired to Annabelle's for a picnic lunch around the pool. As soon as they were able to negotiate it, the cousins slipped away and headed for the woods. They had an hour before they had to return. Their collective excitement grew until they finally reached the clearing. They entered the open space and stared at the caboose.

"Looks the same to me," Quinn said.

"Yeah, except the snow is gone today," offered Chugga. He looked at Annabelle. "And you say your friend Sara couldn't see it?"

"Her name is Stella."

"Sure it is," mumbled Chugga and waited for Annabelle to answer his question.

"This is exactly how it looked yesterday, and no, Stella couldn't see it," declared Annabelle. "If fact," she continued, "not only could she not see it, she and Beau rode right through it."

"What?" said Charlotte. Her brow scrunched up as she thought out loud.

"They rode right through it?"

"That is so awesome!" Quinn said.

"Maybe we are the only ones who can see it. Maybe even the horses can't really see it. Maybe they just sense something is there. That's why they get nervous. They can sense it but can't see it," Charlotte said.

"I wish I could ask them," said Annabelle.

"I wish I could *be* one," Charlotte replied.

"So, like we're the only people who can see this place?" Chugga interrupted. "Or even go into it?"

Annabelle shrugged.

"Maybe."

"That is so dope," Quinn said and began to walk toward the caboose. Charlotte looked at Annabelle.

"Is that a good thing?" Charlotte asked Annabelle.

"Yes. It means it's good."

Henry glanced at Charlotte, who was studying the structure. She felt Henry looking at her and turned toward him. She smiled and nodded. She knew what he wanted to ask her.

"Yep, it feels OK."

Henry nodded and stepped after Quinn. Everyone else fell in after Henry and they all stopped at the stone step. Quinn looked at Henry, who nodded, and Quinn stepped up. The door swung open and Quinn walked in, followed almost immediately by the others.

The interior was completely different from their last visit. There was still a huge table laden with food, but there was also a ping pong table, four flat screen monitors with X Box play stations, three gigantic flat screen TV's with movies playing and a popcorn machine actually popping corn. All of the screens were on, showing movies and video games.

Garrett walked over to the popcorn machine and stared at it as it produced popcorn in huge quantities. Chugga walked over and said, "I gotta get one of those."

Everyone else went straight for the food table, crammed with piping hot hamburgers, hot dogs, pancakes, and much more on one side of the table and cold sandwiches, donuts and buckets of ice cream on the other. Charlotte looked around as she munched on a perfectly made grilled cheese sandwich.

"There's no kitchen here. How did they make all this food?" she asked the group.

Annabelle made a funny face and answered.

"Who is the 'they' you're talking about?"

"Oh, yeah," replied Charlotte. She finished the grilled cheese sandwich and picked up a cookie. She walked away from the table and looked back at the door they had entered. It had closed behind them, and Charlotte marveled at the intricate carvings on the inside of the door. She turned around to go back to the table and stopped in her tracks.

"Uh, guys?" she thought.

Nobody stopped what they were doing, so she changed to voice.

"Hey, guys. Look at this," she almost shouted.

Everyone turned toward her and she pointed at the far wall of the room. They all followed her direction, turning toward the back wall of the caboose. There was a collective intake of air. Lined up along the wall were six golden doors, glistening in the sun shining through the polished sky light in the ceiling.

"Woah." Said Quinn.

As they all stood and stared, black letters began to appear on each door.

"Woah is right," Chugga said as he stared at the doors.

"It's our names," said Annabelle.

"You're right," said Henry. His name was on the first door on the left, and he walked toward it. The others followed, each heading for the door with their name on it. They all paused and looked at each other, wondering who would go first. Garrett answered the unspoken question by reaching up for the gold handle and opening his door. Everyone else followed his lead and opened their doors. There was a collective gasp, then shrieks of joy.

CHAPTER SIX

Chugga was the first to enter his room. It was his dream room, right out of his greatest fantasies. There were posters on all the walls of professional soccer players in action. There was a huge flat screen TV with a play station. There was a twin bed, a table with snacks on it and open shelves with dozens of soccer jerseys. He walked over and pulled one off the shelf and opened it.

"All right!" he said as he held it up. It was Lionel Messi's jersey, and it was autographed!

To Chugga,

Keep kickin'

L Messi

He pulled it on over his shirt and hurried out of the room to show his brothers. He ran directly into Quinn, who was also wearing a new soccer jersey.

"How awesome is this?" asked Quinn, pointing to his Ronaldo autographed jersey. They hi-fived and went looking for Henry. They found him in his room and slipped in. They both stopped in their tracks and stared in amazement. The room looked like a library. Three of the four walls were covered with books from floor to ceiling, and the fourth wall was taken up with a giant telescope pointing out the glass ceiling at the sky.

"Henry, this is awesome!" they both said in unison. Henry just glanced at them and nodded and went back to scanning the books on the walls. Chugga slapped Quinn on the arm.

"Let's go see what's in Garrett's room."

They both trotted out and down the row of doors to Garrett's room, where they found him watching a movie while munching on popcorn. His walls were covered with posters of Batman, Spiderman and numerous other super heroes, and his bed looked like the Bat mobile.

"Great room!" Quinn called out and Garrett waved his hand in the air, dropping a few kernels of popcorn on his head. Chugga snickered and punched Quinn.

"Let's go see what the girl's rooms look like."

They moved out of Garrett's room and stopped outside Charlotte's room. Chugga knocked and Charlotte looked up.

"Hey, Charlotte, can we come in?"

"Sure," Charlotte said with a smile. She was petting a calico cat sitting on her lap, and a parakeet sat on her shoulder watching. The boys entered and looked around. Photos of many different animals were everywhere, and a large bird cage with a number of birds in it filled one corner of the room. Quinn studied the scene in front of him.

"Aren't you afraid the cat will eat one of the birds?" he asked.

Charlotte shook her head.

"No, they all seem to be friends."

Chugga was not convinced and didn't want to be around when the feeding began. He looked at Quinn and nodded toward the door and they both left the room. They knocked on Annabelle's room and she waved them in. She was sitting on the floor petting a small, white, scruffy looking dog that was actively licking her face.

"Isn't he the cutest thing?" she gushed. "I'm going to call him Cozmo."

The boys cautiously petted the dog, looked around the girlie looking room and left. On the way back to their own rooms they peeked in on Garrett again. His room had changed since they were in it a few minutes before. He was sitting in a movie theater type seat watching a cartoon movie on a huge screen. He was eating buttered popcorn and sipping a Coke from a huge cup. He looked at the two when they walked in.

"Hey, guys. Check it out." He pointed a finger at the far wall, where hundreds of DVD's where stacked.

"I've got every movie. All of them."

"Very cool," the brothers said together.

"Have a seat," offered Garrett. "And some popcorn."

"No thanks. We've got to get back."

Garrett shrugged and turned back to the screen.

"OK. See ya."

They two brothers returned to their own rooms and began settling in. Before long their hour was up, and Annabelle was going from door to door, gathering everyone together. No one really wanted to leave their new found paradise, but Annabelle was firm and soon they were all reluctantly closing their doors and lingering in the main room.

They all grabbed a final snack off the food table as Annabelle herded them out the door. Henry took up his now usual place as the final one out the door. He pulled the door closed and started to step down, then stopped. He was curious. What would it look like if he opened the door again? He cracked the door and peered in. The space was totally empty, and there were no doors along the far wall.

"Very weird," Henry said as he closed the door again and followed the rest of the group out of the clearing.

CHAPTER SEVEN

It was raining, so all three Gallahan boys and two neighbors were playing inside. The current game of choice was hide and seek, with Henry designated as the seeker, trying to find Chugga, Quinn and the two friends. The Gallahan home was a four story structure, so there were numerous opportunities for the boys to hide.

Henry called out "here I come," and began his search in the playroom in the basement. By the time he had reached the second floor, where the bedrooms began, he had found both friends, and they were assisting him in the search. He assigned each friend a room and headed for Chugga's room. He knew Chugga liked hiding in his closet and decided to check it first.

Chugga could hear Henry approaching and crawled further toward the back of his closet, trying to find some kind of cover. He reached the back wall and stood up to try to take up less room. As he backed against the wall, he felt something hard against the small of his back. He turned around to see a door with a round door knob.

He closed his eyes and shook his head but when he opened his eyes the door was still there. He heard Henry turning the handle to the closet door and he quickly grabbed the knob in front of him and turned it. The door popped open and he peeked past the door. The room he was looking at was his room in the clubhouse. He jumped in and closed the door behind him.

"This just gets weirder and weirder," he said out loud as he looked around. His stomach grumbled and he decided to see if the food table was in the main room, and if it was full. He went to the door to the central area and opened it. The food table was loaded and he hurried to it and grabbed a chicken leg and a donut. He turned back to the far wall and stopped. His door was the only one along the wall. The space where the other five doors should be was empty.

"Henry, can you hear me?"

"Yeah. Where are you?" Henry replied.

"Go to my room and go into my closet."

"What for?"

"Just do it."

Chugga waited until Henry connected.

"OK. I'm at your closet. Now what?"

"Go inside."

"Why."

"Henry!"

"OK. I'm inside."

"Go to the back of the closet."

"Yeah?"

"Open the door."

"Real funny, Chugga."

"What?"

"There's no door here."

Chugga blinked. This is so weird, he thought to himself. Maybe only I can see the door, just like only the

THE INCREDIBLE COUSINS AND THE MAGIC CABOOSE

cousins can see the clubhouse. Or, maybe I can only see *my* door, but Henry can see one in his own closet!

"OK. Go to your closet."

"My closet?"

"Yeah, in your room."

"No."

"Please, Henry, just do it."

He waited for Henry to climb the stairs to his own room.

"OK. I'm here."

"OK. Go inside your closet, close the door and go to the back of the closet."

"This better be good."

Chugga waited again and suddenly he heard Henry.

"What the heck?"

"Is there a door?"

"Yeah. What's it doing here?"

"Open the door."

Chugga waited a second, then heard Henry's surprise.

"Holy cow! It's my room at the clubhouse."

As Henry entered his room, his door appeared right in front of Chugga in the open area. Chugga smiled. Just as he thought. If he got the others here, their doors would appear in the wall too. The interior of the clubhouse

36

seemed to adapt to whatever was needed by the club members. That was one he'd have to think about. But not now. Ice cream had just appeared on the table, and he was still hungry.

CHAPTER EIGHT

Chugga was on his second bowl of ice cream when Henry came out of his room and joined him at the food table. As he munched on a donut, Henry turned and looked around.

"Looks different."

"Yeah, no kidding."

Henry turned and looked at the wall with the two doors in it. He pointed the donut at the wall.

"What happened to the doors to the other rooms?" he said as he continued to munch on his donut.

"Not sure. I think the doors are only here when the people are here."

Henry nodded.

"OK, I'll buy that."

They ate for a moment in silence.

"Weird place, huh?" Chugga asked as he ran a hand through his mop of blond hair.

"Totally," replied Henry. "But, it's very cool."

He finished the donut and glanced at his watch.

"We'd better get back to our house."

Chugga nodded and started toward his door and Henry followed him. Chugga stopped and turned toward Henry.

"I think we have to go back through or own closets. You couldn't find a door in my closet, remember."

"I guess that's why mom has never seen the door," Henry said. Chugga just shrugged.

"See you at home," he said.

They entered their own rooms. Chugga went to his closet and took a deep breath. Henry hadn't seen a door in his closet at home. He sure hoped Henry hadn't somehow jinxed the door. What if he went into the closet here in the clubhouse and he couldn't get back to the closet at home? What would he do? How would he get home? What would he tell his mom?

He took a deep breath, pulled open his closet door and walked in. He closed the door and moved to the rear of the closet and was very happy to see another door. He paused, then opened the second door and smiled. There was his room at home. Awesome! He flung the door open just as Henry walked into his room.

"Got ya!" said Henry with a grin. They fist bumped and went to look for Quinn.

CHAPTER NINE

The news about the closet connection to the clubhouse spread quickly by teleconnection, and Quinn, Annabelle and Charlotte quickly tried it and returned home safely. The problem turned out to be Garrett. Charlotte explained the process to him, but he balked at entering his closet and closing the door behind him.

"It'll be dark, Charlotte," he complained.

"Will you be OK if I go with you?"

He thought about that for a moment and nodded.

"If you bring a flashlight too."

Charlotte found a flashlight and they proceeded to Garrett's room. She opened the closet door and stepped inside. Garrett hesitated until she turned on the flashlight, and then he wiggled in next to her. It was a tight fit, but they managed.

"I'm going to close the door now, OK?" she asked.

Garrett took a few deep breaths and then nodded his head. Charlotte gently closed the door and took Garrett's hand.

"Let's push your clothes aside and find the door in the back, OK?"

He nodded and they reached the back of the closet with only one step, and Charlotte played the light over the wall. There was no door. She remembered that Henry had said he couldn't find the door in Chugga's closet, but found his own just fine.

"It's not here, buddy. Let's go back out."

THE INCREDIBLE COUSINS AND THE MAGIC CABOOSE

Garrett readily agreed and they hurried out of the closet. Charlotte tried to figure out a way to get Garrett to go back into the closet alone.

"Buddy, the door that goes to the clubhouse is magic. Do you understand that?"

Garrett nodded and she continued.

"But the thing is, it only appears if you are the only one in the closet. If anyone else is there, the door doesn't appear."

Garrett slowly shook his head.

"I don't want to go in there alone."

Charlotte was surprised that he had grasped the situation so quickly.

"What if I stood right outside while you went in, and then ran to my closet and went to the clubhouse to be there when you came out the other side? Can you do that?"

Garrett slowly shook his head.

"I don't want to do that."

"Not even with the flashlight?"

Garrett just kept shaking his head.

Charlotte was silent, trying to figure out what to do. Suddenly she had an idea.

"Hey, where's your head lamp? The one you wear at night."

Garrett's face lit up. He liked wearing his head lamp. He wore it to bed every night. He raced downstairs and quickly returned with the headlamp on his head. Charlotte smiled at him.

"OK. Now, let's turn it on. Then, it won't be dark when you go into your closet. And it's like magic, right? It will protect you. It will be an adventure. OK?"

Garrett nodded.

"Good. So, you go in with your light on, close the door, go to the back of the closet. There will be a door there. Just open it and your room in the clubhouse will be right there!"

Garrett wrinkled his brow.

"How can that be?"

"It's magic, remember?"

"Cool," he said and nodded. He adjusted his glasses and smiled at Charlotte.

"OK. Let's do it. You go in and close the door. I'll run into my room and go into my closet and go into my room at the clubhouse. When you get in your room there, just come out into the living room where the food table is, and I'll be there."

Garrett studied his big sister for a long time. Finally he decided to trust her and nodded.

"OK. See you there!"

He turned his light on, opened the closet door and stepped in. He hesitated for a second, then smiled at Charlotte and closed the door. Charlotte also hesitated, then hurried to her room. She entered her closet and within seconds she was in her room at the clubhouse.

She quickly went out into the main room and looked at the wall of doors. There were no other doors there, and she tried not to panic. What should she do? Go back home? Teleconnect with Garrett to see where he was? A few seconds later Garrett's door appeared in the wall and he stepped out, the smile on his face as bright as the light on his head.

CHAPTER TEN

Two days later, Henry teleconnected with everyone and asked for a meeting at the clubhouse. When everyone arrived, Henry gathered them all in the main room, sitting on comfortable couches that they found there for the first time. Chugga and Quinn were punching each other and Charlotte and Annabelle had their heads together while Henry helped Garrett get comfortable on the couch.

"OK, can we talk a minute?" Henry said. The girls both stopped talking and looked at him, and he was surprised when Chugga and Quinn stopped fooling around. This place really was magic!

"Great. I thought we should talk about a few things. First, has anybody else noticed that when you visit the clubhouse, it doesn't matter how long you stay, when you go back home, only about a minute or two has passed?"

Annabelle responded.

"Yes, which strikes me as curious, especially since it didn't happen the first time we actually entered the caboose."

Quinn nodded.

"That's right. We were a little late getting back to the barn."

"And there was another time when we were here for an hour and an hour passed outside," added Charlotte.

"Right," Henry jumped in. "I think maybe the clubhouse knows it's easier for us to come if no time passes outside while we are gone. The place seems to be adapting to us."

"What do you mean?" asked Chugga.

"It seems to be learning from us."

Charlotte spoke next.

"Yeah, I've noticed that the food table changes a little every time we come, maybe it's trying to find out what we like the best."

"How can it do that?" asked Garrett, his glasses making his big eyes look even bigger.

"Exactly," replied Henry, and continued. "And my room changes a little every time I come, mostly for the better, but still."

"Yeah, my games get cooler every time too'," agreed Chugga. "And when I came in yesterday and saw the basketball court, I was blown away."

"And my room has the cutest little dog," added Annabelle and Charlotte nodded and said "And mine has a cat and a bird."

"Right. So, how is it doing this?" Henry asked.

"You brought us all here to ask us how a magic place does its magic?" asked Charlotte.

"No. I mean, I don't know."

Everyone looked at each other, no one knowing what to say next, so Henry continued.

"Like, what I mean to ask is, what's the deal with this place? How did it get here, and what does it want?"

"It's not like it's a person," replied Quinn. "It's a place. How can it want something?"

"Yeah, but, how does it change itself all the time?" asked Chugga.

"Have you noticed that the food never gets less, no matter how much we eat?" asked Charlotte. "I ate three grilled cheese sandwiches yesterday and the pile didn't get any smaller."

"And doors and windows come and go all the time," added Annabelle.

"And it gave us a superpower," added Garrett.

"Yeah. Good point. I wonder if it can give us more superpowers?" said Quinn.

They all looked at each other and finally Charlotte spoke.

"I wish I could turn into an animal whenever I wanted to."

"Why?" asked Quinn.

Charlotte shrugged. "I just think it would be awesome to be able to be a cat, or a horse, or a bird."

"I think I'd like to be able to talk to animals," Annabelle spoke up after a short pause.

The boys looked at her with blank stares, and then Garrett spoke.

"I want to be invisible."

"That's cool," said Chugga. "I want to be able to time travel."

He looked at Quinn.

"I want to be super strong, and super-fast, and to be able to turn into other objects, and to be able to teleport things, and."

Annabelle broke in.

"Wait, wait. That's like ten things."

"So?"

Charlotte jumped in.

"Maybe just one thing at a time."

"Why? I wanted ten things in my room and they're all there," Quinn argued.

"Yeah," Henry chimed in. "Like yesterday I thought it would be cool to have free vending machines with lots of junk food in my room, and today they're there."

Annabelle glanced at Charlotte, rolled her eyes and murmured "boys." She looked at Henry.

"And what would you wish for if you could have a super power?"

He shrugged.

"I don't know. I think maybe I'd like to be able to regenerate."

"What's that?" asked Garrett.

"Like if I had my arm cut off, I could, like, instantly grow another one."

Charlotte looked at Annabelle and rolled her eyes again.

They continued to talk about their adopted clubhouse, and their wishes, but didn't really come up with any answers. Finally they gave up and slipped back into their own rooms to read, play games, or play with their pets.

CHAPTER ELEVEN

It was three days later before they were all together again in the clubhouse. Henry and Quinn were in Chugga's room playing basketball. All three of them had their own basket to shoot at, and as many basketballs as they wanted. And the best part was, when they tossed a ball, no matter where it went, it bounced right back to the shooter.

"This is so cool," said Quinn as he watched a ball come bouncing back to him. Even though he was over six feet tall, Henry was new to the game, so he was taking tips from his brothers. All of a sudden, all of the balls stopped bouncing and the lights in the room dimmed and then came back up several times. This was followed by soft music floating into the room. The boys looked at each other.

"Sounds like it's coming from the main room," judged Chugga. They all headed for the door to the main room. When they entered the room, they found the rest of the group already there staring at something dancing over their heads.

"What's this?" asked Quinn as they moved closer to the scene. Six lights were swirling over the heads of the group. Chugga stared at the lights.

"They look like stars," he said. "And that's where the music is coming from."

"Yeah. It's like they were calling us into the room," added Charlotte.

"Weird," decided Quinn. "Henry, you're the tallest. Can you reach them?"

Henry reached up toward the stars, but they danced away. He looked around to see if anyone had a better idea.

As they stood there, the stars stopped swirling and settled down, still floating above them. They all studied them and suddenly Annabelle's eyes grew big.

"There are letters on them. One on each star."

Henry started reading them.

"A, Q, H, G, C, and W."

"I think maybe it's the initials of our first names," suggested Charlotte.

"Except who's W?" asked Annabelle.

Quinn quickly figured it out.

"Chugga's real name is Weston. He's called Chugga because Henry couldn't say Weston when he was little. All he could say was Chugga, and it just stuck."

Everyone looked at Chugga and he just shrugged.

"Maybe if we reached for the star with our initial on it, we could get them," said Charlotte.

Henry reached up for the star with the H on it, and held his hand out. The star slowly and gently settled into his hand. It continued to glow as it sat in his hand and he drew it down to examine it. The remaining stars all moved so they were lined up directly over the person they belonged to. Chugga looked at Henry.

"Is it hot? Does it hurt?"

Henry shook his head.

"No. It tingles a little, but it's OK."

Chugga nodded and reached up toward the star with the W on it and it gently settled into his hand. Everyone else quickly followed suit and the music stopped.

"What do I do now, Charlotte?" asked Garrett as he stared at his star. Charlotte shrugged.

"I don't know, Buddy."

"It tingles, like Henry said," Garrett said.

"So, now what?" asked Quinn.

Charlotte began to think out loud.

"Remember the other day when Henry was talking about how this place seems to anticipate our needs?"

Everyone nodded and she continued.

"And right after that we all talked about what if we could have a wish, a super power?" She paused and shrugged.

"Well, these are stars." She looked around and could tell she wasn't getting through. "You know, like when you wish upon a star?"

"Oh, I get it," Chugga said. "We use this star to make a wish, like for a superpower."

Charlotte shrugged. "Maybe."

Chugga held his star up to his face and spoke at it.

"I wish I could time travel."

He stared at the star, but nothing happened. Finally he looked at the others. They were all watching, waiting for something to happen. He looked back at the star, which was still glowing a bright white in his hand.

"Maybe you have to rub it, or something, like a genie's lamp," suggested Quinn.

"It's pretty sandy," piped up Garrett. "So, maybe you're supposed to blow the sand off when you make your wish."

Chugga nodded. Garrett was right. The star did feel a little sandy. He shrugged and looked at the star again.

"I wish I could time travel," he said again, and blew on the star. Suddenly it glowed brighter, then faded to a soft gold glow. The center where the letter W had been changed into a calendar showing the date and time. There were buttons on either side of the calendar. Chugga looked at Henry.

"What do I do?"

Henry looked over Chugga's shoulder at the star.

"Try the button on the left."

Chugga nodded and took a deep breath, then tapped the button on the left. The time flew backward and he stopped. He looked at Henry again as everyone else gathered around.

"Try the other one."

Chugga did and the date flew forward.

"So, it looks like first you pick the time and then the date. The button on the left moves the time or date backward and the one on the right moves it forward," offered Charlotte.

Chugga nodded and worked the buttons again, moving the time and date back exactly one day. He looked up.

"Now what?"

"Try blowing on it again," Charlotte suggested.

Chugga nodded, blew on the star and disappeared.

CHAPTER TWELVE

Chugga had blown on the star and suddenly there was a loud crack and a blinding flash of light. He waited a second for the ringing in his ears to subside and his vision to return. When both senses settled down, he looked around the central room. He was alone. Where did everyone go?

Then he remembered and glanced down at his right hand. It was empty! He tried not to panic, but it wasn't easy. Without the star, how was he going to get back? He reached up and ran his hand through his hair and something scraped against his forehead. He pulled his hand down and looked at it. There was a watch around his wrist. *Where the heck did that come from*, he thought to himself.

He looked at the digital readout on the watch. It read yesterday's date. He looked up quickly. It worked! He had traveled back to the day before. The star had turned into a watch. He had a way back after all.

He looked around the room. The doors of the rest of the group were not there, so he was here alone. Too bad, he thought. If someone else had been there, he could have gotten proof of his travel. Never mind. He looked at the food table. It had just the food he liked on it. He had a quick bite, then decided he'd better figure out how to get back to the present.

He held the watch up to his face and prepared to change the date when he saw a new button that had appeared above the digital readout. It was red and had tiny lettering under it. He moved his face even closer to read the word. It read RESET. He pulled his hand away and considered what it meant. Maybe that was how he was to get back. He considered what to do.

Reset. What would happen if he pushed the button? There was only one way to find out. After all, he couldn't stay in yesterday forever. He took a big breath, held it and pushed the button. The digital read out flashed and changed the time and date to the exact time he had left behind before. He nodded. So it reset to the original time and date. He blew on the watch.

Another loud crack and a blinding flash of light again left him deaf and blind for a moment. When his hearing and sight returned, he was standing exactly where he had been when he left.

"Totally awesome!" he said as everyone gathered around him, asking questions.

"Where did you go?"

"Did it hurt?"

"What was it like?"

Before he answered anyone, he checked his wrist. The watch was still there. He definitely didn't want to lose the little gem.

"I went back to yesterday. I was right here in this room. Too bad none of you were there. It was awesome. I can't wait to go somewhere again. Or, should I say some time?"

After a few more minutes of chatter, the group spread out as each person considered their own star and its possibilities. Charlotte decided she'd like to be the next to try out her magic star. She thought about it for a moment and decided to sit in a chair. She was not surprised to find a very comfortable one that had appeared along the nearby wall, and she settled in. Everyone else gathered around. She leaned forward and studied her star, glowing white in her hand.

"OK. I would like to be a cat. A female cat," she said out loud, but before she could move, Chugga spoke up.

"Wait! I know how you get there, but how are you going to get back?"

Charlotte blinked at him.

"Good question, Chugga."

"Thank you."

"How did you get back?"

"I pushed a button. But you won't have a button, or fingers."

"She won't even have hands," added Quinn with a scoff.

"Yeah," Henry jumped in. "And how are you going to hold onto your star?"

Charlotte looked down at her star and squinted. She held it up to Henry for closer examination. Henry took it from her and nodded.

"I have just what you need in my room. I'll be right back."

He disappeared and returned quickly. He handed the star back to Charlotte.

"There was a small hole in one of the star points. I put a string in it. Put it around your neck."

"Great idea. Thanks."

"She still won't have any hands," argued Quinn again.

"It'll be ok. My star turned into a watch. I'm sure hers will figure out a way to be useful too," replied Chugga.

They all looked at Charlotte and she put the star around her neck, pushed back her long, light brown hair, took a deep breath and spoke.

"I want to be a fluffy black cat, a small female," she said and blew on the star. There was no loud bang or flash of light. Instead, the air around Charlotte seemed to shimmer and she went out of focus, then disappeared. In her place sat the most beautiful black cat the cousins had ever seen, with a tiny silver star on a silver necklace around its neck.

CHAPTER THIRTEEN

Charlotte had closed her eyes when she blew on the star and she kept them closed now. She felt different. Very different. She slowly opened her eyes and almost jumped in wonder. She was looking at her cousins, but they were different too. At five feet six inches, Charlotte was tall for her age, but her perspective now was much lower to the ground. And her vision was unbelievable! She stared at her cousins as if she was seeing them for the very first time, which, in effect, she was.

She stared at Annabelle, seeing things she had never seen before. Everything was sharper, clearer, much more detailed. She could see the sparkle of her long brown hair, her cute, clear eyes. It was remarkable.

And her depth perception was unbelievable. She stretched her taught, strong muscles and stood up, looking at the other cousins. She opened her mouth to say something and almost fell down when she heard the sound that came out of her mouth. For the first time she looked down at herself and jumped straight up into the air. She was a cat!

That's why I see so well, she thought. Cats have great vision. And, with her great vision, she had less fear of moving quickly. She took a few steps, and the sheer joy of it overwhelmed her. She began racing around the room, laughing. But it didn't sound like laughing. She stopped and trotted back to the group.

"Wow," Quinn said as he bent down and petted Charlotte.

"This is awesome," added Chugga. But Garrett wasn't so sure.

"Is this Charlotte?" he asked.

"Yeah," replied Henry. "But don't worry, she can come back as a person whenever she wants." He looked at Chugga and added "Right?"

Chugga nodded.

"Probably all she has to do is say she wants to be herself again, and maybe lick the necklace, or something like that."

They all turned and looked at Charlotte. She wasn't quite ready to switch back just yet. She turned and dashed toward the food table. She leaped into the air and landed on the table.

Awesome, she thought to herself. Right in front of her was a bowl of warm milk. She lapped at it for a moment, surprised at how great it tasted then smelled something overwhelmingly good. She turned and saw a tiny piece of cat nip. She licked it and a jolt of electricity shot through her. She jumped down and ran around the room again, reveling in her new sight and agility.

She returned to the cousins, who were still standing together, watching her. She rubbed against Garrett's leg and he reached down and petted her.

"Hi, Charlotte."

She decided to try to teleconnect with Garrett.

"Hey, Buddy. You OK?"

Garrett smiled and nodded his head.

"Are you going to be Charlotte again very soon?"

Charlotte looked up at Garrett's face and could see the fear in his eyes. She decided she'd better go back.

"I'll be right there."

She ran back to the chair, jumped up and settled down. She thought about what Chugga had said. OK, she thought, I'd like to return to being Charlotte, she thought. Nothing happened. She thought it again and tried to lick the star, but still nothing happened. Everyone was watching and waiting. She decided to connect.

"I don't know what to do."

Everyone looked at each other, not knowing what to tell her. Chugga thought about his experience and got an idea.

"Charlotte. I got back by hitting a reset button on my watch."

"But I don't have any buttons on my star," She replied.

"Maybe the word is the key," Annabelle offered tentatively.

Charlotte nodded. She was getting a little concerned. Being a cat was a nice idea and lots of fun, but she certainly didn't want to spend the rest of her life as one. Even if cats did have nine lives.

She took a deep breath and focused. She pictured the word in her mind and thought **RESET**. The air around her suddenly shimmered and the cat disappeared, and Charlotte appeared sitting in the chair. They all ran to her and Garrett hugged her so tightly she thought he would strangle her. She was happy to be back, but couldn't wait to do it again.

CHAPTER FOURTEEN

Everyone was bubbling with excitement over seeing Charlotte turn into a cat and then return back to her normal self.

"Not something you see every day," Quinn quipped and hugged Charlotte, who was a little embarrassed by the contact.

"How was it?" asked Henry.

"It was absolutely awesome. It was unbelievable how well I could see."

"And how you could jump!" added Chugga with a smile.

"How did it feel?" asked Annabelle. Charlotte launched into a long explanation of feelings, and the guys slowly drifted away. Finally Quinn spoke.

"My turn."

Henry looked at him and nodded. "OK. If you're ready, let's do it."

They moved together to one side of the room and Quinn held out his star. He looked at Chugga for advice, who quickly obliged.

"Just decide what you want and say it out loud, then blow on the star."

"That's it?" asked Quinn.

Chugga shrugged and Quinn nodded.

"I think so," Chugga said.

"Here we go," Quinn said and took a deep breath.

"I want to be able to teleport things," he announced and blew on the star. He stood still and waited. No loud crack or bright light, no shimmering air around his body. Nothing. Was he ready? He looked at Chugga, who just shrugged.

"Try it," Chugga suggested. Quinn nodded and looked around. He focused on the food table. There was a stack of steaming hamburgers and he decided to try them. He reached out his hand, pointing toward the stack and said, "Hamburger, here." Nothing happened. He tried again, this time saying "teleport a hamburger here." Again, no movement at all.

Quinn sighed and visibly slumped. He was clearly dejected. Henry had watched it all and thought he had a suggestion that might work.

"Maybe it only works the other way."

"What do you mean?" asked Quinn.

"I don't know, really. But, maybe you have to, like, touch it or pick it up first, then teleport it."

Quinn nodded and walked over to the food table. He picked up a hamburger and looked over at Henry. He held it out toward Henry and said, "Hey, Henry, hold out your hand."

Henry did and Quinn pictured the hamburger flying to Henry in his mind. He blinked and suddenly his hand was empty and Henry was holding the hamburger, a big grin on his face.

"I did it! I did it!" shouted Quinn as he jumped up and down. Charlotte and Annabelle turned around and looked.

"What happened?" asked Annabelle.

"Watch this," Quinn said and picked up a grilled cheese sandwich.

"Hold out your hand," he said to Annabelle, and she did. Quinn pictured the sandwich flying to Annabelle's hand, blinked and it disappeared from his hand and appeared in her hand.

"That is quite unusual," Annabelle said, examining the sandwich to decide if it had changed in any way and was therefore unsafe to eat. Quinn grinned and started to pick up another hamburger when Chugga rushed up to him, concern on his face.

"Wait."

"What?"

"Where's your star?"

Quinn looked around, but couldn't see the star anywhere.

"I don't know," he answered. "Maybe I don't need it because I don't, like, have to come back from another time, or change back from another form."

Garrett had been standing by watching everything and he spoke up now.

"Look at your hand. You have a new ring."

Quinn looked at his hands, and found a small, thin green ring on the fourth finger of his right hand. He held it out toward Garrett.

"Good catch, Garrett," he said and grinned. "My favorite color."

"I guess maybe it turned into a ring because you have to touch the item before you teleport it," guessed Henry.

"Awesome," replied Quinn. "This is going to be a lot of fun."

"Hey," said Chugga with excitement. "I have an idea. Try this."

He handed Quinn another hamburger and stepped between Quinn and Henry.

"When you send it to Henry, it'll go right through me," Chugga said with a grin. Quinn smiled back, took the hamburger and sent it to Henry. It disappeared from Quinn's hand and appeared in Henry's. Chugga turned around and saw it and whooped.

"That is so cool! It had to go right through me, right? I think I can even taste it!" Chugga almost shouted with glee.

Quinn and Henry both nodded, and Quinn looked around for other things to teleport. Henry felt a tug on his pants and looked down to find Garrett smiling up at him.

"Can I do it next?" he asked.

"Sure," Henry said. "Let's get Charlotte to help, OK?"

"Sure."

Henry called Charlotte over.

"Garrett thinks he's ready to try his superpower out."

"Awesome," Charlotte said and looked at Garrett.

"You're ready, Buddy?"

Garrett nodded his head, suddenly very serious. Charlotte hugged him.

"OK, then. Let's do it. Where's your star?"

Garrett tugged his star out of his pocket and held it out for Charlotte to see.

"Good. So, what do you want as your superpower?"

"I want to be invisible."

"OK. Here's what I suggest. We'll do the stuff to get you to be invisible, but why don't you hold my hand, so we know where you are, just the first time, OK? I'll feel better."

Garrett nodded and took Charlotte's hand.

"Good. And when you become invisible, don't let go, OK? And talk to us so we know you're OK. Got it?"

Garrett nodded again.

"Here we go. Make your wish and then blow on the star."

Garrett took a deep breath and spoke.

"I want to be invisible," he said and blew on the star. Nothing happened. Garrett blinked and looked at Charlotte.

"Am I invisible?" he asked.

"No, buddy. You're still visible."

Garrett sagged.

"Why didn't it work?"

Everyone turned to Chugga, who seemed to understand the power of the stars.

"Well, I think maybe you need to close your eyes before you make your wish."

Garrett nodded, closed his eyes and tried again.

"I want to be invisible," he said and blew on the star. Everyone took a sudden breath, as Charlotte appeared to be holding her arm out in midair, attached to nothing but her own body.

CHAPTER FIFTEEN

At first Garrett was disappointed. It looked like the star thing wasn't going to work for him. Everyone was standing around him and he was still holding on to Charlotte's hand. He tried not to cry. But then he started to pull his hand away from Charlotte and she tightened her grip.

"No, buddy," she said." Remember, we agreed you'd hold my hand while you were invisible". Right? Remember?"

"Yeah, but." Garrett started to object but stopped cold. He was looking at Charlotte's hand, and it was suspended in the air, not holding onto anything. But he could still feel her hand holding his. Annabelle suddenly appeared at his side with a mirror. She held it up so it was facing him.

"Look, Garrett."

He turned and looked into the mirror, and all he saw was the food table behind him. He giggled. It worked! He was invisible.

"Awesome," he said out loud.

Quinn reached out and touched Garrett's shoulder.

"He's right there, but we can't see him."

Charlotte took charge.

"OK, buddy. We know it works. I want you to come back now. We can talk more later about what you can do next time."

"But I want to stay invisible for a while. Can't I just walk around a little? It's no fun with you holding on to me. Everybody knows where I am."

Charlotte was torn. She understood why Garrett wanted to be free for a moment, but was scared that she might not be able to get him back.

"Please, Charlotte?" he begged.

Charlotte sighed and let go of his arm. "Two minutes," she insisted. "Then you come right back here, OK? "

"OK," came the reply from ten feet away. They could hear him running around the room, suddenly stopping at the food table. They watched as a candy bar levitated and its wrapper was torn off. Then it quickly disappeared as Garrett ate it. Then the sound of more running and then the door to his room opened and closed, and a few minutes later opened again.

Then it got very quiet, everyone listening hard, trying to keep track of Garrett. Nobody heard a sound until suddenly Annabelle jumped and squealed as Garrett tickled her ribs.

"Got 'ya!" he giggled, his voice now coming from another part of the room.

"OK, that's enough. It's time," ordered Charlotte. She held out her hand and a few seconds later she felt his hand take hers.

"Now, we are going to bring you back," Charlotte said.

"OK," he said meekly.

Charlotte looked at Chugga.

"I guess he should say reset?" she asked the room in general.

"I guess," Chugga said as he shrugged. "And don't forget to close your eyes, Garrett," he called out to the room.

"Reset," Garrett said in a loud voice, and he was suddenly there in the room again. Charlotte hugged him, relieved that he made it back. Annabelle looked around and then studied Garrett.

"Where is your star?" she asked, concern in her voice.

Garrett also looked all around and suddenly began to cry.

"What's the matter?" Charlotte asked as she hugged him.

"I won't be able to do it again," he wailed.

"Hold on, buddy," Henry said, rubbing Garrett's back. "Let's figure this out. The star turned into something else. Something you can keep with you for when you need it."

Everyone began examining Garrett and his clothes. Finally Quinn spotted something.

"What's that in the corner of his glasses? I don't remember that being there before."

Annabelle peered closely.

"Garrett, can I see your glasses for a minute?" she said.

He carefully took them off and handed them to her. She turned them over and studied the lenses, then held the glasses up to her eyes. She finally handed them back to Garrett.

"Put them on," she said. "I want to show you something."

He did as he was told and then Annabelle spoke again.

"OK. Look to your right, and try to see what's on the inside of your glasses."

Garrett did and smiled.

"It's me."

"Right. There's a tiny mirror on the edge of the right lens of your glasses. So, my guess is, whenever you want to be invisible, you look at your face in the little mirror then close your eyes and say invisible, and it will work," Annabelle guessed.

"And, when you want to come back, you just close your eyes and say reset, and you'll come back," added Chugga.

"And you can always check to make sure you're visible or invisible by looking at the little mirror," guessed Quinn.

Everyone felt good about their collective effort to figure out Garrett's process. Quinn spoke.

"OK. Who's next?"

Annabelle almost raised her hand.

"I'd like to go next," she said a little nervously. "But, first I need to get something. I'll be right back."

CHAPTER SIXTEEN

Annabelle dashed to her room and returned with her small dog under her arm and her star in her hand. Everyone gathered around.

"I'm going to wish that I can talk to animals. It's a wish sort of like Quinn's. I don't have to come back from it like Charlotte or Garrett or Chugga, so it shouldn't be too scary."

"OK, but we still want to be here for you," Henry said. "Just in case."

Annabelle smiled at him.

"Thanks, Henry."

She took a deep breath and said "I wish I could talk to animals," and blew on her star. Everyone watched as she walked to the chair along the wall and sat down with the dog in her lap. She leaned forward and began.

"Hello, Cozmo. How are you feeling today?"

The dog looked up at her, cocked his head to the left and barked. Annabelle leaned back and blinked. She had understood him completely. It was as if he had spoken to her in plain English.

"Really? Where does it hurt?"

The dog barked again and Annabelle picked up his left paw and examined it.

"I don't see any cuts or anything," she said and the dog barked again, and she laughed.

"You were teasing me? That's awesome. I didn't know dogs had a sense of humor."

Annabelle and Cosmo continued an animated conversation for a few minutes until Henry walked over and interrupted them.

"Uh, Annabelle?"

She looked up at Henry.

"So, I guess it works?"

"It's unbelievable. He's so smart, and he's funny too."

Henry smiled as the rest of the group came over and surrounded Annabelle. Charlotte began asking questions that Annabelle relayed to Cozmo and the three of them chatted until Chugga noticed something and asked Annabelle a question.

"So, what happened to your star?"

Annabelle looked around but couldn't find her star until Quinn spotted it.

"Here it is," he said, pointing to Annabelle's left ear. Everyone moved closer and looked. A beautiful small silver star was hanging from a silver pierced earring loop in her ear.

"That makes sense," Henry said. "The stars seem to turn into something that is related to each person's wish. Annabelle has an earring that must translate whatever the animal is saying for her. Charlotte has a necklace that keeps the star near her face so she can always reach it. Garrett has a mirror in his glasses so he can see if he's invisible or not, and Chugga has a watch that tells him the time and date, so he always knows where he is."

"And I have a ring that touches the object I want to teleport," added Quinn. They all turned to Henry and Annabelle asked the question.

"So, are you ready Henry?"

"Sort of," he answered.

"What's the problem?" asked Quinn.

"Well, I want to be able to regenerate, but to do that somebody has got to be hurt first if we're going to see if it works."

"Good point, and I'm not going to volunteer," replied Chugga. He looked at Quinn.

"You could just wait a while until Quinn hurts himself. Shouldn't be long. He's always hurting himself, or somebody else."

It was true. Quinn went about life full tilt, which often ended up with him having a cut, a scratch, a broken bone or some other calamity. Quinn just smiled now, which was also what he usually did when he got hurt. Garrett came to the rescue.

"I have a little boo boo," he said, holding out his right arm. There was a band aid on his forearm.

"Our kitty scratched me when I tried to pick her up yesterday."

"Really?" said Annabelle. "That's unusual. She seems so sweet."

"Well, he tried to pick her up by the tail," explained Charlotte.

"All right!" said Quinn, and the girls both gave him a nasty look.

"Perfect," said Henry. "Let's do this."

CHAPTER SEVENTEEN

Henry took his star out of his pocket and held it up. It was still glowing.

"I wish I could have the power of regeneration," he said and blew on the star. The tingling in his hand disappeared and he looked down at it. The star was gone, but he noticed that there was a band aid wrapped around the fourth finger of his right hand. He held it up for everyone to see.

"I was right. My star turned into a band aid" he said to the group.

They all examined the band aid and Henry turned and looked at Garrett.

"OK, buddy, let me see that scratch on your arm."

Garrett held his arm out and Henry carefully removed the band aid that was covering the scratch on his arm.

"Why are you being so careful with the band aid?" asked Quinn.

"Because, if the regeneration works, the scratch will be gone and his mother probably won't believe he healed that quickly. We'll need to put the band aid back on."

Quinn nodded and Henry handed him the band aid. He looked at the scratch, which was actually three small scratches.

"Hmm. Looks like this hurt."

"Not too much," Garrett said bravely.

"Really?" asked Henry.

"All things are relative," replied Charlotte, knowing that Garrett, like herself, had experienced numerous operations on his eyes in the past, and, compared to that, a few small scratches on his arm ranked pretty far down on the pain scale. Henry peered at the scratches and took a deep breath.

"Well, here goes." He paused and then spoke with authority. "Regenerate."

Nothing happened. Henry stared at the scratches. He looked up at Garrett and back at the scratches. He didn't want to touch them, but maybe he had to be touching Garrett. He took Garrett's arm in his hand.

"Regenerate," he said again, louder this time.

"Maybe you have to touch the scratch," suggested Chugga.

Henry tried it and said "regenerate" even louder. Again, nothing. Annabelle snickered and Henry looked at her, hurt.

"Oh, I'm not laughing because it's not working," she said quickly, sensing Henry was hurt by her laughter. "I just think it's funny that you think saying it louder will help."

Henry stared at her until Garrett spoke.

"It's OK, Henry. It really doesn't hurt very much," he said.

Charlotte had an idea.

"Maybe you have to touch the band aid on your finger, or something."

"Yeah, maybe you have to rub the band aid while you say the word," added Quinn.

Henry shrugged. He'd try anything now. He was embarrassed and frustrated. So, he rubbed the band aid, looked at Garrett's scratch and said "Regenerate" one more time, trying not to say it too loudly. Still nothing. Everyone seemed stumped and Henry was getting very discouraged. Finally Chugga tried another idea.

"Maybe the word is wrong."

"Regenerate?"

"Yeah."

"But that's what I want to do," argued Henry, getting angry.

"Yeah, I know. But when I wanted to return to the present, I didn't push a button that said return, it said reset."

Charlotte chimed in.

"That's right. When I wanted to return to being a human, I said the word reset."

Annabelle summed it up.

"So, maybe try holding Garrett's arm near the scratch with your hand that has the band aid on it, and say the word reset."

Henry sighed, but took the advice. If this didn't work, he wasn't sure what to do next. Everyone else had a superpower except him. It wasn't fair. He took a deep breath, ready to give it one more try. He grasped Garrett's arm so the band aid on his own finger was close to the scratches, closed his eyes and said "RESET". He kept his eyes closed until he heard Quinn say "Yes! You did it!"

He opened his eyes and looked at Garrett's arm. The scratches were gone.

CHAPTER EIGHTEEN

Everyone was very excited about their new superpower and they were talking about them together in the main room. Questions began to pop up.

"Will we be able to use our power outside the clubhouse?" Quinn wondered.

"Let's see," said Henry. "Bring a hamburger," he said to Quinn as he went to the door. They all stepped outside, curious to see what might happen. Henry took a few strides away from the clubhouse into the open field. Everyone followed and Henry turned and faced them all.

"OK, Quinn. Try to teleport the hamburger into the woods."

"Where?"

Henry shrugged.

"I don't know. Just pick out a tree and send the hamburger to it."

Quinn nodded and held the hamburger out and pictured it stuck to the side of a tree he could see at the edge of clearing. He blinked and the hamburger disappeared from his hand and reappeared stuck to the side of the tree.

"Awesome," said Chugga and handed Quinn another burger.

"Try sending it to your room at home," he said and Quinn grinned.

"Great idea," Annabelle said.

Quinn held the burger out and pictured the table next to his bed at home. He blinked and the burger disappeared.

"That is so cool," Garrett said, bubbling with joy.

"I can't wait to see if it's there when we get home," Chugga said.

"I wonder if it will still be hot when you get there," Charlotte said.

"Guess we answered the question about our powers working outside the clubhouse," Henry declared and led the group back inside. When they were all together again, Annabelle looked around.

"Hey, where's Garrett?"

"Right here," Garrett said and giggled. The sound came from right next to Annabelle.

"Garrett, cut it out and come back here, right now," Charlotte said.

"But Charlotte," he objected.

"Right now."

"OK," Garrett said and reappeared. Charlotte instantly grabbed him and hugged him.

"Don't scare me like that again, OK buddy?" Charlotte said.

Garrett nodded and Annabelle asked another question.

"I'm afraid my mom will notice my new earring right away. Do you think I should take it off? I don't really want to."

"Yeah, I don't want to take my ring off either," added Quinn. He looked at Henry for an answer, and Henry just shrugged, not sure at all what to say.

There was no immediate answer from the group, and then Charlotte spoke.

"Maybe we don't have to take them off. Nobody else can see the clubhouse, so maybe nobody else can see the forms the stars have taken. Maybe they're invisible too."

"I bet she's right," Henry confirmed.

"I hope so. I don't want to take it off, but I don't want to have to tell a fib to my mom either," answered Annabelle. She looked at the others and continued.

"I can't wait to talk to Cody, and also to the new horse, Prince Eversoul."

"That's the famous jumper that's boarding at the barn now, right?" asked Henry.

"Yes. He's an international champion."

"Why's he here?" asked Chugga.

"Mister Layman is considering buying him," Annabelle answered.

"Wow!" said Henry. "Why?"

"He just retired, and now he will be put out to stud."

"What does that mean?" asked Quinn.

"Other horse owners who want to have their own champion horse will pay money to have him be the father of a foal they would own."

"Oh,' said Quinn, a little embarrassed.

"Lots of money." Annabelle continued. "Mister Layman is considering buying him, so he's having a bunch of vets check him out to make sure everything is OK."

"If my mom can see my watch and she asks where I got it, I can say I found it in the woods near your house," Chugga said to Annabelle, changing the subject, and she smiled.

Everyone nodded and agreed that would be a good approach if the stars in their new forms were visible to others. They all also agreed to not mention their new powers to anyone else, and reluctantly returned to their own rooms and through them back to their own homes.

CHAPTER NINETEEN

The next two weeks flew by as everyone practiced their new powers, and they all spent hours teleconnecting back and forth about their varied experiences. When summer vacation ended they all headed back to school, some more reluctantly than others. But, since real time didn't move much whenever they visited the clubhouse, they were still able to visit it often.

One day, about three weeks into the school year, Charlotte teleconnected a distress signal to everyone, asking them to meet her at the clubhouse as soon as possible. Within an hour everyone was there, all of them worried.

"What's up?" Chugga asked when they all met in the open room. Charlotte was trying very hard not to cry.

"Someone stole my sketch book," she finally managed to choke out.

"Her favorite one. The one she carries everywhere," Garrett said in support, his big eyes even wider.

Charlotte was a budding artist and she took her sketch book with her everywhere, often drawing things she saw on the spot. She even had a website where she created stories, cartoon type videos, mostly about animals. And she was good. Over the summer she had even taken classes at a Philadelphia art college on a special scholarship and had designed a coloring book that a charitable organization used to instruct children in Africa about the proper treatment of animals.

"Are you sure it's gone?" asked Quinn.

"Positive. I left it in my locker this morning and when I went back at the end of the day it was gone."

"Why would anyone steal a sketch book? Did they take anything else?" asked Annabelle.

Charlotte just shook her head.

"Do you have any enemies at school?" Henry asked.

"School just started. She hasn't had time to make any enemies," replied Quinn. "Besides, how could anyone not like Charlotte?"

Charlotte looked at Quinn and smiled.

"Thanks," she said.

"OK," Henry said. "Let's figure this out. You're sure you put the sketch book in your locker this morning."

"Yes."

"Why?" asked Quinn.

"Why what?" responded Charlotte.

"Why did you take your sketch book to school?" Quinn replied.

"So I could show a few friends what I'm working on."

Quinn just rolled his eyes and Annabelle jumped in.

"I can't believe someone took it. That's terrible, Charlotte."

"I know, right?" she responded, nodding at Annabelle. Henry tried to return the discussion to the issue at hand.

"So, you put it in your locker first thing in the morning. When did you discover it was gone?"

"Not until the end of the day."

"Don't you have locks on your lockers?" asked Quinn.

"Yes, but I don't lock mine."

"Why?" asked Chugga.

Charlotte was embarrassed.

"It's really hard for me to see the numbers on the lock."

Chugga felt terrible for asking and tried to quickly move on.

"OK. So, did you tell anyone at school?" he asked.

"Like who?"

"I don't know. Like your teacher, or a hall monitor."

"Well, yeah. I told them all."

"What did they say," Henry jumped in.

"Not much. Basically, they said I should lock my locker."

"Big help," muttered Quinn.

"Are there security cameras in the halls?" asked Annabelle. Charlotte shook her head.

"I don't know."

"Why don't you check that out tomorrow," Annabelle suggested.

"And ask your friends if they saw anything or if they have any ideas," added Chugga.

"Then let's meet here again tomorrow and see what we can figure out."

Everyone snacked a little from the food table and gradually moved back to their own rooms. Before he left for home, Chugga went to Charlotte's room. He knocked and went in when Charlotte said "come in". When he entered he stopped. One entire wall of the room was glass, but what stunned him was what he saw out the window.

"Is that for real?" he asked and pointed toward the window.

Charlotte looked up and saw he was pointing outside.

"Oh, well. I figured out that the clubhouse gives us whatever we want in our room, so I asked for a view of a giant bird sanctuary. Pretty cool, huh?"

Chugga stared at the jungle outside the window and saw dozens of macaws, parrots, hummingbirds, and many more birds he couldn't identify flitting right outside the window.

"But this isn't real," Chugga objected. Charlotte looked at him and scoffed.

"Oh, and flying hamburgers, invisible kids and a girl that can turn into a cat is real?"

Chugga nodded.

"Good point. I gott'a go."

He turned and rushed back to his own room, and within minutes he had a huge glass wall with a view of the ocean. He looked at it and nodded.

"Very nice," he decided. He took a few more shots with the endless supply of basketballs, grabbed a few snacks from his own food table and headed for his closet.

CHAPTER TWENTY

The club met again after school the next day.

"Any luck today?" asked Henry when they were all gathered in the main room.

"Yes, and no," replied Charlotte. She rummaged in her back pack and pulled out a thick black book. Quinn whopped.

"You got it back?"

Charlotte nodded, but looked very sad.

"So, what's the matter?" asked Chugga.

She thrust it out at the group in general.

"Look."

Annabelle took the book, opened it and turned a few pages.

"Oh, no," she gasped and turned more pages, then held it out for the group to see.

"Someone scribbled on every drawing."

"That sucks," offered Henry.

"Seriously," agreed Quinn. "Let's go find the guy and."

"Quinn," interrupted Annabelle with a sharp look and he stopped and shrugged.

"Where did you find it?" asked Henry.

"It was in my locker this morning when I got to school. I went early. "

"Really?" said Chugga, who found it hard to imagine anyone would want to go to school earlier than they had to.

"Any idea who did it?" asked Annabelle.

"None at all," Charlotte said as she sadly shook her head.

"Must be somebody who has it in for you," guessed Quinn.

"But who?" Charlotte said, trying not to cry.

"Someone who is maybe jealous of you," suggested Annabelle.

"How can we find out?" said Henry.

"I checked about the security camera thing, and there aren't any," Charlotte said.

"Maybe Chugga could go back to the day you lost it and watch your locker to see who did it?" suggested Quinn.

"Except I can go back in time, but not in a different place. At least I don't think I can," replied Chugga.

"Plus, the person might not do it if Chugga is standing right there," added Annabelle.

"And how would he know the right time to go? He can't stand there all day," said Charlotte.

"Hey!" Chugga almost shouted and everyone looked at him.

"I have an idea. I could go to your house, and go back to the day before you took the book to school. I could get it and hide it so you couldn't take it to school with you the next day. Then this would never happen," he said to Charlotte.

"That's a great idea," Charlotte beamed at Chugga. "When's the next time you're coming to my house?"

"I don't know. Maybe get your mom to invite us over this week end and I can do it then."

"Awesome. Thanks everybody!" Charlotte beamed. The group chatted a little more, then broke up to return to their homes.

CHAPTER TWENTY ONE

Charlotte worked her magic with her parents and the Gallahan family was invited to visit the following week end. All three of the boys were in her room, along with Garrett. The door was closed as Chugga was preparing to time travel.

"OK. Where did you keep the sketch book last week?"

Charlotte pointed at her dresser.

"Top drawer, right side."

"Are you sure?"

"Positive."

He looked around the room.

"I'll need to hide it somewhere so you won't find it until I show you today where it is when I come back."

Charlotte looked around the room and shrugged.

"OK."

"We need to leave so we don't see you hide it, right?" asked Henry.

"I don't think so, because you won't be here, but I guess it won't hurt."

"Yeah. Let's go," Quinn agreed. Chugga set his watch while everyone else filed out of the room. Charlotte leaned in and whispered, "Good luck," and closed the door, leaving him alone. He put ear plugs in his ears, put on sunglasses, took a deep breath and blew on the watch. Following the loud clap and bright light, he opened his eyes. Everything looked pretty much the same. He shook his head.

"Man, she's neat," he said and walked over to the dresser. He opened the top drawer and found the sketch book right where Charlotte had said it would be. He pulled it out and opened it. No slash marks.

"Great," he said and closed the drawer. He had an idea and he held the book in his hand. Maybe not only could he time travel, but anything he held in his hand could go with him.

"Reset," he said and returned to the present. The book was still in his hand. He looked at Charlotte's desk and the damaged book was gone. He opened the door and found everyone standing in the hallway.

"All done," he said and opened the door wide. Everyone quickly moved in and Charlotte looked at him expectantly. He smiled and handed her the undamaged book.

She took the book, looked inside and gave Chugga a hug.

"You're the best."

He smiled, a little embarrassed.

"No problem."

Charlotte showed the book to everyone and they all nodded approval.

"Good job, Chugga," Henry said.

"I still think we should have tried to find out who took it," added Quinn.

"Just don't take it to school again," suggested Henry.

"No way," agreed Charlotte.

"Well," said Quinn. "I guess we can go home now."

Charlotte smiled.

"I think you're invited for lunch."

"OK," Henry said and they all went downstairs to join the grown-ups.

CHAPTER TWENTY TWO

After two weeks as a freshman in high school, Henry had discovered a secret that changed his life. Well, at least his after school life. Homework was burying him until he discovered he could do it in a breeze in his room at the clubhouse. He could read difficult chapters in minutes and understand and remember everything. He could do algebra problems in his head and he could write excellent reports and papers as fast as he could type.

He had just finished his homework and walked out of his room into the living room, as they now called the large common room in the clubhouse. He glanced at the wall and saw that Quinn's door was the only other one there. He walked to the food table and picked up an icy cold Coke and looked around.

Annabelle suddenly teleconnected with him.

"Anybody at the clubhouse?" she asked.

"I'm here," Henry responded.

"OK. Good. I'm riding Cody and we're on our way."

"I'll be here." Henry responded.

He looked around again. Something was wrong, and he noticed it instantly. There were no windows on the wall. He sipped his Coke and walked over to the wall. It felt colder near the wall and he reached out and touched the wall, then jerked his hand back. The wall was freezing.

"This is weird," he said out loud. Where did all the windows go? And why was the wall so cold? He reached out and touched it again and it was not only cold but felt hard as steel.

"I wish I could see outside," he said out loud and suddenly a tiny hole appeared directly at his eye level. He stepped forward and put his eye to the hole. He could only see part of the clearing and the trees at the far end of it. There was something there. He squinted to try to make it out, but couldn't. Some sort of dark shape was in the woods.

He peered longer and the shape slowly cleared up. It was a person, maybe in a long black robe with a hood. He kept staring and the shape continued to clear up until he could actually see the eyes peering out of the darkness of the hood. They were green and they were staring right at him.

Suddenly the eyes flashed brightly and Henry was knocked backward. He stumbled and almost fell. It was almost like something had pushed him. He looked back at the wall and the small opening was gone.

"Quinn! Quinn, come here. In the living room. Quick!" He teleconnected. Quinn's door opened and he walked into the room.

"What?" he said, and stopped when he saw Henry's face.

"This is really weird," was all Henry could say.

Quinn looked around and spotted the blank wall.

"Where'd all the windows go?"

"There's someone out there," Henry said.

"How can you tell? There are no windows."

Quinn walked to the wall and looked back at Henry.

"Tell the wall you want to see out. But be careful. Whatever it is knocked me backward," Henry explained.

Quinn nodded and looked at the wall.

"I want to see out."

A small hole appeared at his eye level and he stepped forward and put his eye directly in front of the opening. As he looked at the clearing and then the woods, he saw the shape.

"I can see a shape, but I don't know what it is," Quinn reported.

"Keep looking. It gets clearer."

Quinn kept staring and the shape slowly became a figure in a dark robe with a hood.

"I got it now. I see somebody in a robe wearing a hoodie."

"Watch out. It'll flash at you."

Quinn continued to stare. The green eyes appeared under the hoodie and flashed at him. He flinched but didn't fall backward.

"That was weird," he said and continued to stare at the shape. The shape went out of focus and cleared again. The green eyes flashed again, brighter this time, and again Quinn flinched but still did not move back.

"What is it?" Henry asked. Quinn stepped back and the hole disappeared.

"I don't know. But it had really bright green eyes that flashed at me."

"I know. I saw them too. It was scary."

Suddenly Henry remembered Annabelle. She was coming right toward the mysterious figure. He had to warn her before she got too close.

"Annabelle! Listen to me. Don't come near the clubhouse."

"Why not?"

"There's someone here that is scaring us. Stay away. Go back to the barn."

"OK."

Henry stepped forward and spoke.

"I want to see out again."

A hole opened in the wall and he stepped up and peered out. The shape was gone.

CHAPTER TWENTY THREE

Everyone was gathered in the living room listening to Henry and Quinn excitedly describe what had happened to them. When they finished the group began a barrage of questions.

"Was it a man or a woman?"

"What did it want?"

"Where did it come from?"

"Where did it go?"

Henry raised his hands.

"Wait, wait. One at a time."

He looked around the circle. Everyone was sitting on large bean bag chairs that were there when they all entered the living room. He tried to answer the questions one at a time.

"I couldn't really tell if it was a man or a woman. It was in the shadows and the hood over its head didn't help any."

He glanced at Quinn, who just shrugged as he answered.

"I have no idea. It was not real tall, so maybe a woman, but I don't know."

Henry nodded and continued.

"I think the next question was, what did it want? I don't know that either. It just kept staring at the clubhouse."

"But I thought nobody but us could see the clubhouse," Chugga said.

"I know, but it sure looked like the thing was staring at it," Henry replied.

"Yeah," Quinn added. "With really weird looking green eyes. They were the only thing I could see under the hood it had on. And when they flashed it felt just like somebody was trying to knock me down. It was very strange."

"None of this is rational," offered Annabelle. Henry looked at her with raised eyebrows.

"What part of what happens in this place is ever rational?"

Annabelle paused and stared at Henry.

"Excellent point," she replied and Henry continued.

"I saw the green eyes too, and they pushed me backward when they flashed."

"I'm a little scared," Garrett piped up and Henry reached over and patted him on the shoulder.

"It'll be OK. We won't let anyone hurt you," Henry reassured him.

Garrett peered at Henry and nodded. Charlotte spoke for the first time.

"I think we will have to assume that this person has some super powers just like we do. Maybe even stronger, which means it may have gotten them from the clubhouse before we found it."

"And," added Annabelle. "Maybe it's come back and wants the clubhouse back."

"I'm not giving this place back to anyone. It's way too cool," Chugga said.

"So, what do we do?" asked Henry. The group was quiet, each person trying to come up with an idea. Finally Quinn spoke.

"The next time it comes by, I'll go out and try to talk to it."

Charlotte shook her head.

"I don't think that's such a great idea. You don't know what powers it might have."

"I don't think the clubhouse will let it in," responded Henry. "We'll be safe inside."

Annabelle spoke again.

"I agree. The clubhouse sensed its presence and didn't want to let it in. That's why it made all the windows disappear and the wall in front got really hard. It was protecting itself."

"And the wall was really cold too," Quinn added.

"Yeah," replied Charlotte. "That's very interesting. Maybe it knows that cold is a good defense against this witch."

"We don't know it's a witch, or even a female," Annabelle said.

"A witch works for me," Quinn said, rubbing his forehead where the flash from the green eyes had given him a headache.

"But I think we do need a plan," added Chugga.

"OK. Let's all agree that we won't come here alone anymore. At least not until we can figure this thing out," Henry said.

"And we won't go outside if it's here," cautioned Charlotte.

"We can try to communicate with it without going outside," agreed Annabelle.

"Maybe it can teleconnect, just like we can," said Quinn.

"Good idea," replied Henry. "The next time we see it, we can ask who it is and what it wants and see if it can hear us."

"OK. Excellent plan. But right now I have to go. It's dinner time," Annabelle said.

"How do we know it won't get in here while we are gone," asked Garrett.

They all looked at each other and Annabelle spoke as she stood.

"I think it can't get in."

"Maybe that's why it was so mad," guessed Quinn.

"Will it hurt us?" asked Garrett.

Chugga put his arm around Garrett and smiled at him.

"No. It won't hurt you."

Garrett smiled and Charlotte took his hand. They all finally said their good byes and hurried back to their respective homes, each as anxious as the others about this new alarming situation.

CHAPTER TWENTY FOUR

The scary shape in the woods didn't show up the next few times the group gathered at the clubhouse, and gradually things slipped back to normal. One day they were all gathered, Chugga and Quinn shooting hoops, Henry reading, Garrett playing video games, Charlotte drawing in her sketch book and Annabelle talking to Cozmo.

Quinn and Chugga took a break and went into the living room for a snack. Quinn picked up a hot hamburger and studied it. He looked at Chugga.

"I've been thinking."

"That's a scary thought," Chugga replied and Quinn punched him on the arm.

"Ow. That hurt."

Quinn just smiled.

"Anyway. If I can teleport anything I want, why couldn't I teleport myself?"

"I don't know. I guess you could."

"It's a little scary, you know. Henry says that all the molecules in the object separate, disappear, and then get back together again somewhere else."

Chugga thought about it and realized what Quinn was worried about.

"Oh, yeah. What if, like when you got back together, your head was attached to your knee, or something?"

"Seriously."

They both contemplated the cosmic consequences. Finally Chugga ended the silence.

"Let's ask Charlotte and Annabelle."

"Good idea."

They called both of the girls out of their rooms and explained the question.

"Well, that is an interesting physiological question," Annabelle said with a furrowed brow.

"I agree," Charlotte said. "Why don't we do an experiment?"

"Like what?" asked Quinn, cautiously.

Charlotte shrugged.

"Let's find something alive and you can teleport it and we can check it to see if everything is in the right place when it arrives."

"Good idea," Chugga said. "What should we use?"

They all looked at Charlotte as she considered the problem.

"Something that's a little more complex than a bug."

"How about Cozmo?" asked Quinn.

Annabelle paled and clutched the dog tightly to her body.

"Absolutely not!"

"Ok," he said with his hands up in the air. "Sorry. Not Cozmo."

"We need, like a mouse or something," Charlotte said, looking around. Within seconds the clubhouse delivered a small white mouse in one corner and Quinn spotted it. He dashed over, scooped it up and brought it back to the group.

"Now what?" he asked. Annabelle spoke.

"Let's put some markings on it. That way we can check it afterward to make sure everything came back together correctly."

"Good idea," Chugga said and Charlotte dashed into her room and returned with a handful of colorful markers. They marked the mouse's shoulders, L and R in green and drew a straight red line across its tummy and a blue circle on the top of its head.

"That should do it," Charlotte judged and handed the mouse to Quinn. He stroked its head to calm it, then teleported it across the room. They all ran over and Quinn scooped it up and held it out for Charlotte to examine. She checked everything out and announced a successful test. Everyone looked at Quinn and he nodded.

"OK. Here we go."

Before he could begin, Henry came out into the living room.

"What's going on?"

"Quinn's going to try to teleport himself," Chugga explained.

Henry's head snapped toward Quinn.

"Are you sure? We talked about this, remember?"

Charlotte explained their test and the results and Henry shrugged.

"OK. Let's do it."

They all turned to Quinn, who smiled, focused on a chair that had appeared against the far wall, and disappeared. Everyone turned and looked at the chair, where Quinn was sitting and smiling. They all ran over and he jumped up and they all hugged.

"You did it!" shouted Chugga.

"Are you OK?" asked Henry.

"I'm fine. In fact, I feel great!"

Just then the final door on the wall opened and Garrett walked into the living room.

"What's going on?" he asked and everyone laughed.

CHAPTER TWENTY FIVE

It was the weekend before Christmas and they were all gathered at Nana and Grandpa's home, a large converted stone barn. They had eaten and exchanged presents, and now the grownups were sitting around the fire in the living room and the cousins were all gathered in the loft, their favorite spot in the barn.

The loft had its own bathroom, bunk beds, a TV, skylights and a balcony. But, best of all, you could look over a chest-high wall down into the living room, which allowed you to spy on the grown-ups. Henry and Charlotte were spying while the rest of the group was playing various games. To keep from being spotted, they were teleconnecting.

"Wow, people really look funny when you see them from right above, huh?" Henry said.

"I know, right?" Charlotte replied.

The grown-ups were clustered into three groups. Grandpa and Nana were talking with Grandpa's mother directly below them, the three dads were off to the right, and the three moms were huddled around the fireplace.

"The ceiling is so high in this room that it's hard to hear what they are saying," complained Henry.

"I know, it echoes up here. I just try to concentrate on one area. It seems to help a little," Charlotte replied.

"You know, you really shouldn't be listening into other people's conversations," a voice burst into both their heads. They jumped back and looked around.

"Who was that?" asked Charlotte.

"I don't know. It sounded like a grown-up to me," replied Henry.

"Don't you even recognize your own Grandpa's voice?"

"Oh, my gosh, Grandpa? Is that you?" Charlotte asked.

"Yes."

"I didn't know you could teleconnect!" Henry said.

"Is that what you call it these days?"

"That's what we call it," replied Charlotte.

"Who is we?"

"The cousins. Well, at least the cousins that are your grandchildren," answered Henry.

"Interesting," the voice came from behind them. They jumped and turned around to see their grandpa standing there. He quickly touched his finger to his lips and switched back to teleconnecting.

"I'm a little rusty at this. Haven't done it in years. Not since my grandpa died when I was in college."

"There's nobody else for you to connect with?" asked Henry.

Grandpa shook his head.

"It seems to skip a generation. I could talk with my grandpa, but not with my parents. And, for some reason, neither of my sisters could do it. Not my kids, your parents either."

"That's sad," replied Charlotte.

Grandpa just shrugged.

"It is what it is."

By this time the rest of the cousins had heard the conversation and had all gathered around. Grandpa looked at all of them.

"Can you all do it?"

Everyone nodded and he laughed out loud.

"This is so cool!"

Then suddenly his face got serious.

"Wait. How did you all get this power?"

They all looked at each other and Garrett answered.

"From the magic train in the woods."

"It's here?" Grandpa asked, shocked.

Everyone nodded, surprised that Grandpa knew about the train.

"Near our house, in a clearing in the woods," Annabelle said.

"You know about the clubhouse?" asked Chugga.

Grandpa nodded.

"Yeah, except it was on my grandfather's farm in Indiana when I last saw it. Between two small ponds behind the corn field."

"I thought grownups couldn't see it?" Quinn asked.

"I was a kid then. Not sure if I could see it now. Haven't seen it for over forty years."

Everyone looked at each other and Grandpa connected again.

"Does it still look like a ratty old piece of crap?" He asked.

"Looks like a dump," replied Quinn.

Suddenly Nana's voice floated up from the kitchen.

"OK everyone. Time for ice cream and cake."

Grandpa looked at everyone.

"We'd best go down stairs." He put his finger to his lips.

"We'll talk more later. But nothing more now, OK?"

Everyone nodded and they all went down stairs for cake and ice cream.

CHAPTER TWENTY SIX

The cousins couldn't wait to show Grandpa their clubhouse, but it didn't happen right away. It took almost a week to coordinate a time when everyone could make it. The hardest part was, Grandpa didn't have access through a closet in his home like the rest of them did. They hoped that might change once he visited the clubhouse.

Grandpa arrived at Annabelle's house early on a Saturday morning under the guise of wanting to go for a walk with her. He chatted briefly with her parents and then he and Annabelle set out, talking quietly once they were away from her parents.

"So, when did you find the caboose?" Grandpa asked.

"The day of my birthday party."

"Really. And you've all been able to keep it a secret since then?"

"It's actually not so hard. Nobody else can see it, and we can go to it whenever we want by just going through a secret door in our closets. And, when we're there, no matter how long we stay, it's only a few seconds later when we come back home."

"Fascinating," he replied. "And that's where you learned how to teleconnect?"

"Yes. And each one of us got a super power there."

Grandpa stopped walking and stared at her.

"Seriously? You all have a superpower?"

Annabelle nodded.

"We got to pick. Stars appeared with our initials and gave us the power we asked for." She showed him her earing.

"Do you have a super power too?" she asked.

"Yes."

"What is it?"

"I'll tell you later, when we're all together."

Annabelle was a little disappointed. She wanted to be the first to know, but Grandpa was probably right to wait to tell them all together.

"Do you have a star?" she asked.

He shook his head. "Not really. I have a lump on the back of my head." He bent down and rubbed a spot. She reached up and rubbed where he indicated.

"Oh, yeah. That's sort of gross."

Grandpa just shrugged.

"Nobody knows about it, so it's OK."

They had reached the clearing and Annabelle stopped and looked at Grandpa to see if he could see the caboose. He stood and stared at it so long she was afraid he couldn't see it, but finally he spoke.

"I can't believe it. It's exactly like I remember it." He looked at Annabelle. "But I remember snow around the base."

"Oh, the snow kind of comes and goes," she replied.

"Let's go inside," Grandpa prompted.

They walked up to the door and it popped open. Annabelle smiled at the sight. The clubhouse was welcoming Grandpa. She went inside first and Grandpa followed and stopped to look around.

"It's all a lot more up to date than when I was here last," he chuckled.

"Can I call the others and ask them to come. They've been waiting."

"Sure."

Annabelle teleconnected with the others and they all arrived within minutes and a party broke out in the living room.

"The food is certainly better than the last time I was here," Grandpa noted as he spooned a hot fudge Sunday. They then took turns showing Grandpa their own rooms and when they returned to the living room they discovered that there was a door for Grandpa on the wall of doors.

"Awesome!" said Quinn. "Can we go in?"

Grandpa nodded. "Sure," he said and opened the door. He stopped cold before entering. The room was small and decorated according to his tastes when he was a teenager. It was like walking into a time warp. Posters of his favorite baseball players from the sixties, and a device that looked exactly like the radio his engineer father had made for him from scratch when he was twelve. A stack of forty five records sat next to an old hi-fi record player, and a black and white TV was on, showing a baseball game.

"Wow!" said Chugga. "This is like a museum." Grandpa just nodded and walked into the room.

"This is like a dinosaur TV," Henry quipped.

"Nothing has changed since the last time I was here," Grandpa said, smiling.

"What happened back then?" asked Charlotte. "Why did you stop coming?"

"Well," said Grandpa as he walked around fondly touching items. "This place was on my Grandfather's farm, and when he died and we all went to the funeral, I went out to where it had been, and it was gone." He shrugged and sat down in the one chair in the room.

"I just assumed it all had something to do with him, and since he was gone, so was the caboose," he said a little sadly.

They could all tell this was very emotional for Grandpa, so they were quiet. All except for Garrett, who walked up to Grandpa and tapped him on the knee.

"I can be invisible. Want to see?"

Grandpa laughed.

"If you can be invisible, how can I see?"

Garrett thought about that for a moment and then smiled.

"You can see me when I come back."

Grandpa patted him on the arm.

"Sure. If you want to show me, that would be great."

Garrett promptly disappeared and reappeared thirty seconds later.

"I can't do it much faster than that," he apologized.

"That's OK. That was great!"

Garrett beamed and suddenly everyone wanted to show Grandpa their super power. First Chugga picked up a pencil and a piece of paper off the small desk in the room and handed it to Grandpa.

"Hold this," he said. Grandpa took the paper and Chugga traveled ahead thirty seconds, wrote 'Hello Grandpa' on the paper and returned.

"Now, watch the paper," he said and a few seconds later the words appeared on the paper.

"How'd you do that?" asked Grandpa appropriately amazed.

"I went a little into the future and wrote on the paper."

"Awesome," was all Grandpa could say.

Then Charlotte turned into a cat and sat on Grandpa's lap, Annabelle brought Cozmo into the room and chatted with him, Quinn teleported another hot fudge Sunday from the table to Grandpa and Henry regenerated a few scratches Grandpa had on the back of his hand from putting up the Christmas tree.

"This is all fantastic," Grandpa admired when they were all finished. Garrett stepped forward and peered at Grandpa.

"Do you have a super power too?"

"Actually, I do," he said, pausing and looking around at all of them. "I don't use it much, especially when anyone else is around. I've never had anyone like you I could tell about it. So, it'll have to be our secret, OK?"

Everyone nodded agreement at once. They all knew Grandpa was very smart, and they imagined he had thought up a very unusual super power. They couldn't wait to hear what it was. But, before he could tell them, there was a loud bang from the living room, and the entire clubhouse shuddered as if it had been hit by a wrecking ball.

CHAPTER TWENTY SEVEN

Everyone dashed into the living room. Henry was the first to react.

"Oh, no. It's back."

"What's back?" Grandpa asked.

"The windows are all gone. The last time that happened there was something outside at the edge of the clearing," Quinn added.

"It was shaped like a person, dressed in a black cape with a big hood on top. It was staring at the clubhouse," Henry said.

"Yeah," Quinn continued. "And its green eyes flashed and it felt like someone was pushing me, real hard."

"How could you see it without any windows?" Asked Charlotte.

"Just walk up to the wall and say you want to see out. A small hole appears right at your eye level," Henry answered.

Charlotte started to walk toward the wall but Grandpa reached out and grabbed her arm.

"No, wait, Charlotte. I'll look."

Grandpa walked toward the wall and Henry warned him.

"Be careful, Grandpa. Don't touch the wall. It's really cold."

Grandpa nodded and stopped a foot away from the wall. Everyone watched, waiting to see what Grandpa would do, but he just stood very still for almost a minute, then turned back toward them, a very worried look on his face.

"What's wrong, Grandpa?" Garrett asked.

"Why didn't you look outside?" Annabelle asked him.

Grandpa stayed quiet for another moment, then looked up at the group.

"I did look out, just not through a hole in the wall. Don't ask for any more holes in the wall. She may have figured out a way to get in through a hole, even a small one."

"Who?" asked Henry.

Grandpa sighed, paused for a moment and then made a decision.

"Is there someplace we can all sit down?"

Annabelle pointed to a corner of the living room where two couches and several chairs had appeared. Grandpa nodded and they all sat down.

"OK. The thing you saw outside is a...." he paused, as if trying to find a better word than the one that was on the tip of his tongue.

"Well, she's a witch."

They all looked at each other and Garrett scooted closer to Charlotte on the couch.

"How do you know that for sure?" asked Chugga.

"I recognized her."

"How could you see her?" Charlotte asked.

"I used my super power." He paused and explained. "I call my super power 'me two'. The easiest way to explain it is, anything that I can do with my body I can do with my mind."

He looked at the group and saw confusion on their faces.

"OK, suppose I want to eat another hot fudge sundae, but I don't want to leave this chair to get it. In my mind I picture my body going over to the food table and getting the sundae and bringing it back."

He looked over at the table and everyone followed his eyes. They all watched as a hot fudge sundae lifted off the table and floated over to Grandpa, settling into his hand.

"So, just now when I wanted to see what was outside the caboose, so I pictured my body out there and just looked around. I saw the figure you were talking about at the edge of the woods, so I walked right up to it and looked closely."

"And you could see it?" asked Garrett.

"Yes."

"And you recognized it?" asked Henry.

"Yes. She hasn't changed very much. Well, that form of her that's out there now hasn't changed much. She can change into a lot of different looks, but the one she's in now, the cloak and hood, is her natural state. Her name is Hexa."

"How do you know her?" Annabelle asked.

"She tried to take the caboose away from me, a very long time ago."

"And you had a fight with her about it?" Quinn asked.

"Sort of."

"And you won," Chugga said.

"Well, let's just say that she went away, and I never saw her again."

"And now she's returned and she wants the clubhouse," surmised Annabelle. Grandpa nodded and continued.

"I think it might actually have been hers in the beginning. At least that's what she claimed when we were fighting over it. She said she found it on the West Coast and she said she was the one that gave it magic powers. But I got the feeling that the caboose didn't like what she was doing in it. So it closed up once when she went out and it moved. I think that's how it got to Indiana, which is where I found it."

"Wow, this is so cool," Quinn said.

"So, how did she find it here?" asked Annabelle.

"I have no idea," replied Grandpa.

"And how did it get here from Indiana?" asked Chugga.

"Again, I have no idea," Grandpa said.

"Why did it come here?" asked Henry.

Grandpa looked at each one of them slowly before answering.

"I think because you are all here," he said and paused. "Remember when I said the superpowers in my family skipped a generation? Well, I think it came looking for you because it's your turn to share the powers of this place."

"What are we going to do about her?" asked Charlotte, nodding her head toward the outside.

"Well, first of all, you all need to stay away from her if you can. Let me think about it."

"That's OK with me," said Annabelle.

"Me too," Garrett added.

Grandpa slapped his knees and stood up.

"But first, I have to figure out how to get out of here. I don't think the caboose will let any of us out the front door as long as the witch is out there."

"Let's go into your room and see if there is a door in your closet," suggested Chugga.

"Good idea," answered Grandpa, and they all filed into his new room. Grandpa spotted a closet in the corner of his small room.

"This was never here before," he said as he stepped up and opened the closet door and peered inside.

"I don't see a door."

"It's not there until you close this door," offered Garrett.

Grandpa nodded.

"OK. I'll be right back," he said and closed the door. Everyone waited and about a minute later Grandpa opened the door again and stepped back into his room. He smiled at them all.

"Wow. This is very cool. There is a door in the back, and when I open it, I'm in the closet in my bedroom at home."

Everyone grinned as Henry said "Welcome to the cousin's clubhouse, Grandpa."

"You should have a name for it," he replied.

"Good idea," Henry agreed.

"How about the pirate's den," Chugga offered, and both girls wrinkled their noses. Quinn saw it and replied with a smirk.

"How about the tea club house."

"Do you mean T as in tea or T as the first letter of the?" Annabelle asked.

"If we did initials we could call it 'CC'" Charlotte added.

"Why not 'CCH'", asked Chugga.

"Because clubhouse is one word," answered Annabelle.

"Oh," was all Chugga could reply, somewhat embarrassed.

"CC's sounds OK. Like, meet you at CC's in five minutes," decided Henry.

"It sounds a little sissy to me," complained Quinn.

"Deal with it," Annabelle replied.

"CC's. I like it," Grandpa said, and the name was decided.

CHAPTER TWENTY EIGHT

They all went home and gathered again the next morning in the living room at CC's. They grabbed snacks from the food table and settled into chairs and on couches, all looking at Grandpa as he munched on a bowl of buttered popcorn.

"So, how is everyone today?" he asked as he grabbed a frosty bottle of Coke and took a sip.

They all answered positively, and then grew quiet, waiting for him to continue.

"Well, any questions?"

"Yeah," said Quinn. "Does Nana know you have superpowers?"

"Yes, she does. It would have been hard not to tell her. I get too lazy sometimes when she asks for something or when I want something and I send 'me two' to get it. Hard to hide that."

Everyone smiled.

"What about when you were a boy?" asked Chugga. "Did your mom and dad know you had super powers?"

"Not that I know of. But, I have to say that my mom didn't miss much, so maybe she knew and didn't say anything. Mothers tend to know everything, you know."

"Tell me about it," said Quinn and Charlotte giggled.

"I told Nana about what happened yesterday. She wishes she could come too, but the door wasn't there when she came into the closet with me. She thought I was teasing her."

"Yeah," Garrett said. "Charlotte couldn't come into my closet either. I had to go in alone."

"Were you a little scared the first time?" Grandpa asked.

Garrett nodded and Grandpa smiled.

"Me two," he said and Charlotte pushed him.

"I get it. 'Me too'. Good one, Grandpa."

Annabelle spoke up next.

"Do you know why time doesn't change while we're in the clubhouse?"

"I have no idea. I don't actually remember if it did for me when I was a kid. But, I think it's a very cool thing."

Quinn spoke next.

"Can you really go anywhere you want?"

"As 'me too'? Pretty much," Grandpa replied with a nod.

"Like, can you go to my house and tell me what my mom is doing right now?"

"Sure I could, but how would you know if I was right or not?"

"Good point," Quinn replied. "But, maybe you can go into my room at home and tell me something about it?"

"Sure," Grandpa said and was quiet for a few minutes.

"Wow, you cleaned up. The bed is made and everything."

Quinn grinned and Grandpa asked "Where do you keep your money?"

"In my wallet."

"Do you know how much you have in it right now?"

Quinn nodded.

"Pretty much."

"OK, where is it?"

Quinn glanced at Chugga and then whispered to Grandpa "In the top drawer of my dresser, under my socks."

Grandpa nodded, then said "Got it. Let's see, you have twenty, forty, sixty, seventy, five, six seven. Seventy seven dollars. Right?"

Quinn's eyes got big.

"That is so dope."

Grandpa frowned and leaned over toward Charlotte. He whispered to her.

"Is that a good thing?"

Charlotte rolled her eyes.

"I think so. It's a guy thing."

Grandpa nodded.

"Any more questions?" he asked the group, looking around.

"Yeah, what are we going to do about Hexa?" Henry asked.

"I don't know. How often has she been here?"

"Only twice, I think. At least while we've been here," Henry answered.

"Why can't she get in?" asked Annabelle.

"The caboose won't let her. It takes away the windows and seals the wall against her," Henry replied.

"Why does it get so cold?" Garrett asked.

"I think maybe it makes the wall harder," Grandpa guessed. "But I don't know for sure."

"Couldn't she just go around the back?" asked Chugga.

"I don't think there is a back," answered Grandpa. "At least there didn't used to be one."

"What do you mean?" asked Annabelle.

Grandpa stood up. "Let's go out and I'll show you."

"But you said we shouldn't go outside," Garrett reminded Grandpa.

"That's true. When I'm not here, I don't think you should go outside. But, 'me too' just looked outside now and I didn't see Hexa anywhere, so I think it's safe for us right now."

They all stood and followed Grandpa out the door. He gathered them a few yards in front of the caboose and they all faced it.

"OK. Have any of you ever been around to the back?"

They all looked at each other and collectively shook their heads.

"That's because there is no back. It's always the front."

"What do you mean?" asked Chugga.

"That's not possible," added Charlotte. "Everything is three dimensional."

Grandpa shook his head.

"As I recall, if you walk to the end of the front of the caboose and turn the corner, you'll be at the front again."

They looked at him as if he'd grown another head.

"Here, let's try an experiment. Henry, you and Garrett stay here with me. Chugga and Charlotte will go to the left and Annabelle and Quinn will go to the right. When you get to the end of the caboose, turn the corner. OK?"

Everyone nodded and the two groups set out while the third group stayed put.

"Stop for a second when you get to the corners," Grandpa called out and they did. When they were both ready, he nodded.

"OK, go around the corner."

Both groups did and a second later they each appeared at the opposite side of the front of the caboose from where they had just left. They stopped and stared at Grandpa and his small group standing there. Charlotte turned around and went back the way she had come and appeared back on the other side of the front of the caboose next to Annabelle and Quinn. Grandpa called out to her.

"Charlotte, this time don't go all the way around the corner, just poke your head around."

Charlotte did as he said and the group all laughed. They could see Charlotte's back on the left side of the caboose and her head peeking around the corner on the right side. Grandpa waved them all back to the middle.

"That's how the caboose defends itself. It can concentrate all of its energy in one direction. It doesn't have to worry about four sides, because it doesn't have four sides."

"But inside it does," protested Garrett.

"Aha!" said Grandpa. "But inside it is also much bigger than outside, right?"

"Right," Garrett agreed.

"So, how does it do it?" asked Chugga.

"I have no idea," answered Grandpa, shaking his head. They all stood for a moment looking at the caboose, then Grandpa spoke again.

"Let's go back inside. I'm hungry," and they all followed him inside.

CHAPTER TWENTY NINE

It was Saturday morning, Henry's favorite part of the week. His high school began classes at 7:30 in the morning, which meant he had to get up around 6:00 in order to catch the bus at 6:50. Since Henry was not a morning person, his mom let him sleep in on the week-ends to catch up.

He was doing just that when suddenly his head exploded with sound.

"HENRY! HENRY! HELP ME, HENRY!"

He jerked himself awake and groaned.

"What now?" he mumbled as he tried to pull himself awake.

"HENRY! I NEED HELP!" Shouted the inside of his head.

"Annabelle, is that you?"

"Henry. You have to come, quickly."

"Calm down. What's the matter?"

"I was riding Cody out in the field behind the barn and he tripped on something and fell. He broke his leg, really badly and it's bleeding. You have to come help him."

He stumbled out of bed and began to quickly dress.

"OK, I'm coming."

"Cross the clearing and come straight out of the woods. We're just on the other side."

He was hopping on one leg trying to get his pants on as he replied.

"Can't you get help from the barn?"

"It's too far away, and I didn't bring my phone. I'm afraid he'll bleed to death."

He threw open his closet door and stepped inside, still tugging at his shoes.

"OK. Hold on. I'm coming."

He rushed to the back of the closet, but there was no door there. He blinked and realized he had not shut the other door. He turned, closed it and turned back. The door was there and he opened it and stepped into his room at the clubhouse. He dashed across his room and burst into the living room and stopped cold. The outer wall was closed and there was ice on it. The witch must be outside, he reasoned.

"Oh, no, not now," he groaned out loud and stepped up to the wall. He started to tell the wall to let him out when the wall shook with a heavy sound as something slammed into it. He stepped back and tried to think. There was no other way out of the clubhouse. He did the only thing he could think of.

"GRANDPA, WE NEED YOU!"

There was no answer, so he calmed down and tried again.

"Grandpa, I know it's early, but we have an emergency."

"What's up, buddy?"

Grandpa sounded sleepy. Henry realized he had been holding his breath. He let it out now and explained.

"Annabelle just connected me. She was riding Cody and he fell. He's hurt real bad and she needs me to help him. I'm at the clubhouse but the wall is up and I can't get out."

"Hold on one second. Let me look."

Suddenly 'me two' arrived at the edge of the clearing and looked around.

"OK. The wall is up because Hexa is there, about ten feet from the front door. Whatever you do, don't tell the wall to let you out." Grandpa teleconnected with Henry.

"What am I supposed to do? Annabelle thinks Cody might die." Henry replied.

"Hang on a second," Grandpa said as he used 'me two' to assess the situation. Hexa was staring intently at the wall, which was slowly adding ice to its outer surface. As the ice grew closer to her, she slowly retreated.

"She must hate cold" Grandpa said as he watched. Suddenly the witch balled her hands into fists, brought them up by her head and thrust them at the wall. Huge balls of fire flew out of her hands and crashed into the wall of ice, making a sound like thunder and an explosion of fire and blinding white light like a lightning strike. Deep holes were burned into the wall of ice, but it quickly repaired itself and continued its slow advance toward her.

"HENRY! HURRY!" connected Annabelle.

GRANDPA! HURRY!" Henry connected, passing on Annabelle's urgency.

"OK, OK," replied Grandpa.

'Me too' slipped around behind the witch, stopping ten feet behind her. He took a deep breath and charged toward the witch. When he reached her he threw his arms around her and began pushing her toward the ice wall. Since 'me two' was a projection of Grandpa, he was the same size, which was six feet two inches tall and about 190 pounds, and, despite his age, still in pretty good shape.

His size, strength and surprise were all too much for Hexa and she stumbled forward. 'Me two' kept pushing until they both hit the ice wall. The witch let out a blood curdling scream and began thrashing wildly, tryng to get free of 'me two'.

The thunderclap when the witch hit the ice was deafening, and steam began to pour out from the spot as fire met ice. 'Me two' held on as long as he could, and suddenly there was a brilliant flash of light and the witch disappeared. 'Me two' almost fell when the resistance of the witch's body was gone. He quickly stepped away from the ice wall, which was already receding. Within seconds the ice was gone, leaving only a pile of snow along the base of the clubhouse.

So that's where the snow comes from, Grandpa thought to himself.

The windows appeared in the wall and the door swung open. Henry paused a moment and Grandpa coaxed him out.

"It's OK. She's gone."

Henry still hesitated until his head exploded again.

"HENRY! HURRY!"

The pain in Annabelle's voice built a fire under Henry and he dashed out the door. He looked around for Grandpa, but saw nothing.

"I'm here, but you can't see me. Hurry up. You're the only one who can help Cody."

It was freezing outside and Henry only had on a lightweight shirt. He had forgotten to dress for outdoors. He dashed back inside, hoping he had a coat in his clubhouse bedroom and wouldn't have to go home to get one. He almost fell as he crashed into a chair sitting just inside the door. Hanging from the back of the chair was a black ski jacket. Henry grabbed it and slipped it on. It fit perfectly. He raced back outside and dashed into the woods, hoping he wouldn't be too late.

CHAPTER THIRTY

Henry burst out of the woods onto the field and stopped, scanning the area for Annabelle. He heard her voice to his right.

"Over here!"

He looked around and saw Cody lying on the ground, Annabelle sitting next to him, her arms wrapped around his neck. Henry dashed over and stopped when he got close, trying not to get sick from the sight. Cody's right leg was lying at an odd angle and there was bone sticking out of a huge open wound. Worst of all, though, was the blood spurting out of the wound. The bone had obviously severed an artery on its way out.

"Oh, man," Henry said as he dropped to his knees next to Cody. He hated the sight of blood. He glanced at Annabelle and saw the tears rolling down her cheeks. He looked more closely at the injury and tried to control his roiling stomach. He took a deep breath.

"It's going to be OK, but I think I'll have to do this in stages."

He leaned forward, trying to avoid the blood spurting out onto the ground.

"OK. Tell Cody this first part will maybe hurt, but I'll be as fast as I can."

Annabelle whispered into Cody's ear and looked back at Henry and nodded. He reached forward and grasped the leg, one hand on each side of the shattered bone.

"Bone, reset!" he said loudly. The bone slipped out of focus for an instant and when it became clear again, it was totally healed.

"Yes!" Henry said and sat back on his haunches. He took a sharp breath as a white hot pain shot through his leg. He closed his eyes until the pain subsided. He glanced down at his arms and legs. He was totally covered in Cody's blood.

"OK, now we're going to stop the bleeding," he explained and Annabelle whispered again into Cody's ear. The horse looked at her and then at Henry, his big eyes pleading for help. Henry took another deep breath, leaned forward and grabbed the area where the blood was spurting out of the leg.

"Blood vessels and arteries, reset," he intoned. The blood instantly stopped spurting and Henry let the air out of his lungs. Again he felt pain, but this time not as sharply.

"One more thing to do, and I think we'll be done," he said to Annabelle and moved his hands around the still open wound.

"Skin, reset," he said and the wound completely closed. He sat back again, suddenly exhausted. He looked at Annabelle.

"I think that's it."

Annabelle whispered to Cody, who grumbled something back to her. She looked up at Henry.

"Cody says thank you very much, but he's still very tired and weak."

Henry nodded and studied the area again. Suddenly he heard Grandpa's voice in his head.

"I bet he's lost a lot of blood."

Henry nodded and looked around him. He was covered with blood and the ground was red everywhere.

"I think I'm going to have to try to replace the blood," he said to Annabelle. He thought about it for a second.

"Tell Cody I'm going to hug him and replace his lost blood."

Annabelle whispered into Cody's ear and he seemed to nod. Henry leaned forward and spread his long arms around Cody's deep chest.

"Blood, reset," he said and held on. Cody shuddered noticeably, then calmed down. Henry leaned back and almost passed out. Clearly, the regeneration had taken its toll on him. He sat on the cold ground and waited until the dizziness went away and then stood up. Finally Cody stood. Annabelle stood with him and they kept their heads together for some time. Then she looked at Henry.

"Cody says to tell you he feels fine now. He says to thank you for saving his life. He was afraid he was going to die."

"Can't let that happen now, can we?" Henry said, trying to hide the pride he felt. He looked down at the ground again, and was almost sickened by the sight of all of the blood. He started to look away, but something caught his eye. He stared closer at the mixture of blood and snow. There was something shiny lying there. He bent down, pushed some snow away and picked up the shiny thing. It looked like a piece of glass, or a mirror that had broken off a bigger piece of something. It was in the perfect shape of a triangle, almost like a giant arrowhead. He started to throw it away, but something told him to hang on to it. He shrugged and stuck it in his pocket.

"I'm proud of you, buddy," Grandpa said in Henry's head.

"Thanks, Grandpa," he replied.

"Grandpa is here?" asked Annabelle.

"I needed him to help me get out of the clubhouse. The witch was back."

Annabelle thought about that for a moment and then replied.

"Maybe she was the one that tripped Cody. Maybe she knew I would call you and she was trying to get into the clubhouse when you came out of it to help me."

"But how would she know what our super powers are?" replied Henry.

"Let's talk about it later. I'm going to get Cody back to the barn. He needs to rest."

"OK."

"Thanks Henry. You're the best."

"Hey, no problem."

"And thanks, Grandpa."

"Glad I could help."

Annabelle mounted Cody and headed back toward the barn. Henry watched her go, then looked down at himself. He was covered in blood.

"Oh man, what a mess."

"You'd better get cleaned up before you go home," Grandpa said.

"But how?"

"Take a shower in your room."

"But I don't have a shower in my room?"

"Really?"

Henry thought about it for a second.

"You're right. There's probably already a shower there. But what about my clothes?"

"My guess is, you can shower with them on and they'll be clean and dry by the time you get to the closet."

Henry nodded and turned toward the clubhouse. As he walked he continued to talk to Grandpa.

"Thanks for coming so fast."

"No problem."

"What are we going to do about the witch?"

"We'll have to have a meeting. I have some ideas."

"Can't you get rid of her for us? You did it before."

"I don't think so. I think you and your cousins will have to do it without me."

"Why?"

"I just think that's how it works. The clubhouse belongs to you now."

"Great."

"Don't worry. You are all smart and strong. You'll figure it out."

Henry walked the rest of the way to the clubhouse trying not to think about the challenge that lay ahead.

CHAPTER THIRTY ONE

Annabelle came home from school a few days later to find her mother in the barn talking to a woman Annabelle had never seen before. She dropped her back pack in the house and wandered out to the barn to check on Cody. It was cold but a lot of the horses were turned out. She found Cody out in one of the fields and gave him a big hug.

"*What are you doing out here?*" she asked.

"*It's my turn in the rotation to be out,*" Cody replied.

"*Are you cold?*"

"*No. It's not too bad out today.*"

"*Who's the new lady mom is talking with?*"

"*Someone who wants riding lessons.*"

"*Oh.*"

"*We don't like her.*"

"*Who doesn't?*"

"*Me and the other horses.*"

Annabelle pulled away from Cody and looked him in the eye.

"*Why?*"

"*She's scary.*"

"*But you just saw her for the first time today, right?*"

"*Yes, but she makes us all nervous.*"

Annabelle looked back at the barn. Her mom was standing outside holding the reins of Rocky and talking with the woman. Rocky was pawing the ground and seemed anxious.

"*Maybe I should go check her out,*" Annabelle thought out loud.

"*OK, but be careful. Don't go anywhere alone with her.*"

"*You're being silly, Cody.*"

But when she looked into his eyes, she could see that he really was afraid.

"*OK. I'll be careful.*"

"*Promise?*"

"*Promise.*"

She patted Cody on the neck and walked back to the barn. As she walked she tried to study the woman talking to her mom. They were about the same height, but the woman was heavier, more rounded. She had dark, medium length hair and was dressed in bright colors. When she got closer to them, her mom called out to her.

"Hey, Annabelle."

"Hi, mom."

"How was school?"

"OK."

"Come say hi."

Annabelle walked up to the two and patted Rocky on his nose.

"Hey, Rocky."

He gave her a forlorn look and she rubbed his nose again as her mom spoke.

"Annabelle, this is Miss Henderson. She's going to be taking riding lessons here."

Annabelle turned toward the woman, who spoke in a scratchy voice.

"Hello, Annabelle."

Annabelle looked up at the woman's face and took a sharp breath as she peered into the piercing green eyes staring back at her. Now she understood why Cody and the other horses were afraid. And so was she.

CHAPTER THIRTY TWO

Chugga and Quinn were in Chugga's room shooting hoops and talking about how best to use their super powers.

"I was thinking maybe I could go into the future to when we get a test back from the teacher. I could try to memorize the answers, so when I came back to the present and took the test, I'd get them all right," Chugga said.

"Wouldn't it be easier to just study in the first place?" countered Quinn.

"Maybe, but it would be a lot more fun to do it the other way."

"I was thinking it would be cool if I could teleport myself back and forth to school," Quinn said.

"Why? You'd get there sooner."

"Yeah, but I wouldn't have to take the bus, so I could sleep later."

"But what would you tell mom why you weren't taking the bus?"

"Oh, yeah."

They shot for a while in silence until they both heard Annabelle teleconnecting.

"Is anybody at the clubhouse?"

"Yeah," connected Chugga. *"Me and Quinn."*

"Good. I'll be right there. Don't go anywhere, OK?"

Chugga looked at Quinn and shrugged and they continued shooting until Annabelle knocked at the door.

"Come in," called Chugga, and Annabelle entered.

"Hey," Quinn said as Annabelle watched.

"That is really cool," she said.

"What?" asked Chugga.

"How the balls bounce back to you after every shot."

"Yeah, it was Quinn's idea."

"But, don't you get more exercise if you have to chase the ball?" she asked. They both looked at her as if she had three heads.

"Never mind," she said. "Can we talk?"

"Sure," Chugga said and as he continued to shoot.

"Without you playing ball at the same time," Annabelle said sharply.

Chugga's shoulders sagged as he turned toward her.

"OK. Let's grab a snack in the living room."

They all three went into the living room, selected snacks from the food table and sat down.

"What's up?" Chugga asked.

"There is a new lady taking riding lessons at the barn."

Chugga shrugged.

"So?"

"I think it's the witch."

"What?" Quinn said, alarmed. "How do you know?"

"I don't for sure. But she has weird green eyes and all of the horses are afraid of her."

"That's not good," Chugga offered.

"Duh," Quinn said.

"Why would she want riding lessons?" asked Chugga.

"I don't know."

"Maybe to try to get close to you. Become your friend. Ask you to bring her here?" guessed Quinn.

"This is really not good" added Chugga, shaking his head.

"What should I do?" she asked.

"I don't know. Maybe we should get Henry and Charlotte here and get their ideas on the subject," suggested Quinn.

Just then Annabelle's phone buzzed. She picked it up and checked it.

"A text from my mom. I've got to go."

She jumped up and looked at the boys.

"Maybe we can get everyone together tomorrow after school to talk about this," she said.

"Good idea," agreed Chugga.

She turned to go and Quinn spoke.

"Hey, Annabelle. Be careful."

"For sure," she said and went back into her room. Chugga looked at Quinn.

"Shoot some more hoops?"

"Sure."

CHAPTER THIRTY THREE

Everyone gathered the next day after school to talk about the appearance of the witch as a normal person asking to take riding lessons.

"Are you sure it was the witch?" Charlotte asked.

"Not positive. But, she had really scary green eyes and all of the horses are afraid of her."

"What do they say about her?" Henry asked.

Annabelle shrugged.

"They can't explain why they are afraid. They just say that she makes them very nervous and that they feel like she would hurt them if they did something wrong. None of them want to be alone with her."

"Well," Quinn said, "sooner or later we're going to have to figure out how to get rid of her."

"Yeah," agreed Chugga, "but how do we do that? The only time we've seen her so far has been when she's outside the clubhouse. And we can't even get out to go talk to her."

"So, maybe it's a good thing that she is taking lessons. At least we might be able to talk to her while she's in normal form," Charlotte said.

"I don't want to talk to Hexa," Garrett said in a quiet voice. "I don't like witches."

Chugga looked at Garrett and smiled.

"Don't worry. If she starts to try to hurt you, you can just become invisible and she won't be able to find you!"

Garrett looked up at him and smiled. "I think you're right."

"So, what do you think I should I do?" Annabelle asked the group.

"Maybe we should try to talk to her when she's there taking a lesson," Quinn suggested.

"Are you crazy?" asked Chugga.

"No. Listen. If she's taking a lesson from Annabelle's mom, I don't think she will try to do anything scary in front of her. Maybe we can talk to her and figure out what she really wants."

"Who's going to talk to her?" asked Henry.

Quinn shrugged.

"She doesn't scare me. I'll talk to her."

"Nobody scares you," Charlotte commented and Quinn just smiled.

"But you don't have any reason to be at the barn. You don't ride," argued Annabelle.

Quinn was quiet, trying to think of a good reason to be at the barn. Annabelle finally spoke up.

"Oh, well. I think you're probably right. She wouldn't try anything with my mom right there. I can try to talk to her."

"Yeah, and if anything bad happens, you can just teleconnect with me and I can teleport there to help you out."

151

"You don't know what kind of magic she might try to use," cautioned Chugga.

Quinn just shrugged again. He really wasn't afraid of anything.

CHAPTER THIRTY FOUR

Several days later one of the stable helpers called in sick so Annabelle was mucking stalls to help out her mom. She was talking to the horses as she cleaned each stall, and she was having a great time. She was particularly intrigued by the stories Prince Eversoul had to tell of his travels around the world. She knew how famous he was and asked him why his current owners were interested in selling him. He told her he was getting too old to compete at the top level and so he recently completed his last year of competition.

"But you are still a very valuable horse," Annabelle argued.

"Yes, but about the same time as I finished the circuit for the year, my owner died. Her husband isn't really into horses, which is why he's been shopping me around."

The story made Annabelle sad.

"That must be hard for you."

"The hardest part has been the loss of my owner. She and I were very close. But at least I got to meet you. You're the first human I've ever met who can understand me. It's very nice."

She rubbed his nose and smiled.

"It's pretty cool for me too."

"Who are you talking to?" a voice asked from behind. Annabelle jumped at the sound and whirled around to find Miss Henderson standing at the door to the stall. She took a sharp breath and tried to remain calm.

"Oh, hello, Miss Henderson," she said in as calm a voice as she could muster. "I didn't hear you come in. How are you today?"

The woman stared at Annabelle through slitted eyelids and a shudder ran down Annabelle's back. Prince Eversoul moved around behind Annabelle and almost whispered to her.

"Be careful of this one," he warned and she nodded without thinking. Miss Henderson cocked her head.

"What did he say?"

"Who?" asked Annabelle, trying to look as innocent as possible.

Miss Henderson stared intently at her for another moment, but then she glanced away and the spell was broken.

"Never mind. I have a lesson today. Can you help me saddle up Rocky so I'll be ready when your mom comes out?"

The last thing Annabelle wanted was to be close to the woman, but she couldn't figure out a way to gracefully say no.

"Sure. Rocky's right over here," she said and led the woman to the next aisle and down to Rocky's stable. When she arrived she found Rocky at the back of the stall, looking nervously at the door.

"Hi Rocky," Annabelle said with as much cheer as she could muster. "Time for your lesson."

Rocky eyed her and answered.

"I don't want to go out with her."

Annabelle didn't know what to say, so she just opened the door and walked in.

"Come on, big guy," she said as she guided him out of the stall, slipped a bridle on him and secured him to the wall. Miss Henderson stood behind her as she worked.

"I suppose you expect me to learn how to do all of this," she said.

"Yes. I will show you this time, but next time you should try to do it by yourself," Annabelle answered. She tried to keep her mind clear in case the woman could read minds.

"Do you ever give lessons?" Miss Henderson asked hopefully.

"No, just my mom."

"Oh, well. Maybe you and I could go riding sometime when I get a little better at it."

"Maybe," replied Annabelle.

"I'd love to ride around the property. I hear there's a nice woods in the back."

Annabelle glanced at her and shuddered. She was dressed in gaudy clothes just like the last time Annabelle had seen her. Wild colors that didn't really go together, as if she had no style or color sense at all. Or, as if she hardly ever wore regular clothes at all.

But, what made Annabelle shiver was her eyes. They seemed to glow as she stared at Annabelle, probing her as if she was trying to get inside Annabelle's mind. She tried to ignore the feeling.

"I don't get to ride much at all during the school year, what with school and homework and music practice," Annabelle said.

"Well, hopefully it will work out sometime. I hear there's a beautiful little clearing in the woods, and I'm afraid to ride that far alone."

Annabelle turned and stared at the woman. She was smiling back at her.

"You know the clearing I'm talking about don't you, dearie?" She said, her eyes flashing. "There's a very unusual structure sitting right in the middle of the clearing. Have you seen it?"

Fortunately, just then Annabelle head a voice over her shoulder.

"Hello, Jean. How are you today?"

It was Annabelle's mother. Annabelle breathed a sigh of relief.

"Thanks for helping tack up the horse, Annabelle. Next time Jean should do it by herself, OK?"

"Sure, mom. I finished mucking the stalls. Can I go in now? I've got lots of homework."

"OK, honey," her mom replied. Annabelle looked at the woman.

"Good bye, Miss Henderson," she said and tried not to run as she left the barn and headed for her house. As she hurried across the parking area toward her house she looked around at the cars parked there.

"I wonder where she parked her broom," she muttered to herself and then she almost ran toward her house.

CHAPTER THIRTY FIVE

It was Friday evening and Chugga was playing basketball in the township league. His team was down by five points at the half, and Chugga was not happy. His dad was talking to him, trying to get him into a more positive mood.

"Chugga, it's OK. You're only down five. Plenty of time to come back."

"But dad, Sean is hogging the ball and taking bad shots."

He was right, but there was nothing much his dad could do about that.

"Just be patient, and when you get the ball, play your game. You're a good passer and shooter. Just let it happen."

The second half started and things didn't get much better. Henry and Quinn were in the stands with their parents. Neither was particularly interested in the game. Quinn was sitting with his back against his mother's side, reading a book and Henry was studying the small crowd watching the game.

He spotted a woman sitting by herself at the end of the bleachers and was moving on to the next person when something clicked in his head. He swung his gaze back to the woman and took inventory. She was older, short dark hair, a little frumpy looking. He couldn't figure out why his brain had drawn him back to her when she suddenly looked in his direction.

Henry took a sharp breath and quickly looked away. He pointedly watched the game action, all the while aware that a pair of eyes was boring into him. The same pair of striking green eyes that he had seen at the edge of the woods. He decided to connect Annabelle.

"Annabelle. It's Henry."

"Hey, Henry. What's up?"

"You told us the other day about a woman taking riding lessons at your barn, and you're pretty sure it's the witch, just looking different than what Quinn and I saw in the woods. Like a normal person, right?"

"Yes."

"What exactly does she look like when she's looking normal?"

"Middle aged, almost old. Short, dark hair, overweight. Why?"

"There's a woman here at Chugga's basketball game, and she's staring at me."

"Does she look like what I described?"

"Yeah, sort of. But lots of women look like that to me."

"So why are you connecting with me about this one?"

"I think it might be the witch in a different disguise."

"Why do you think it's the witch?"

"Her eyes. They're a weird green. The only time I've ever seen eyes like that was when I saw the witch outside the clubhouse."

There was a long pause. So long, in fact, that Henry thought maybe he'd lost contact with Annabelle. But then she spoke.

"Maybe she can change and look different whenever she wants."

"But why is she here?"

"Maybe she's trying to get close to all of us in different ways, trying to find a way to get into the clubhouse."

"Yeah, maybe. OK. Thanks."

"Sure. And Henry?"

"Yea?"

"Be careful."

"Thanks."

Henry turned to his left and Quinn was staring at him.

"Did you hear?" Henry asked him.

"Yeah," Quinn replied and looked around. *"That woman over there?"*

"Yeah."

"I'm going to check it out."

Henry started to object, but Quinn was already up and walking toward the woman, who was now watching the game again. He sat down next to the woman and waited. Finally she turned her head to look at him.

"Hi." Quinn said.

"Hello," the woman said with a small smile playing at the edges of her mouth.

"Do you have a son playing in the game?" Quinn asked, following a pattern he had heard his mother use when she was trying to meet people at the sporting events she attended so frequently.

"No. I just like watching basketball," the woman replied.

"They're not very good in this league. If you really like basketball, you should watch high school or college. They're much better."

She looked back at the action as she asked her next question.

"You have a brother playing out there now, don't you?"

"Yeah. The tall guy in the middle, dark hair, number fourteen," Quinn said.

The woman turned and stared at him for an uncomfortably long time.

"Really? That surprises me. I would have guessed you were related to number eight, the boy with the long blond hair."

He had intentionally described the wrong person to see what she would say, and was not surprised at her answer.

"Nope. You got it wrong," he said with a straight face, returning her stare with one of his own. She slowly smiled.

"A strong one, aren't you?"

Quinn returned her smile with one of his own.

"Very," he said, then stood up and walked back to his family.

CHAPTER THIRTY SIX

An hour later Charlotte was performing in a musical at her middle school. Garrett was sitting in the first row of the audience with his parents, and enjoying every minute. At intermission his dad asked if he wanted a treat and they went to the foyer behind the theatre for a snack. Garrett selected a bag of M&M's and his dad asked him if he needed to go to the bathroom. He nodded and they walked through the crowd to the boy's room.

"Do you need me to come in with you?" his dad asked.

Garrett shook his head.

"No, thanks. I can do it. I'm big now."

"OK," his dad answered and pointed to a group of people a few yards away. "I'll be over there talking with those people. They're friends of mine."

Garrett nodded and slipped inside. When he was finished he came back out. The space seemed much more crowded than before, and he couldn't see his dad right away. He started to walk through the crowd, trying to find his dad. He was bumped by a teenager running down the hall, then kept going.

He was getting a little nervous when suddenly a woman bent down in front of him, blocking his way.

"Are you OK, young man?" she asked in a sweet voice.

Garrett looked up at her, but didn't recognize her. He peered at her, trying to bring her into better focus, but without success. He guessed she was about the same age as his mom, with the same long, brownish hair. She had very bright colored clothes on, and when he didn't answer right away, she asked again.

"Can I help you find your Daddy?"

Garrett cocked his head. How did she know he was looking for his dad? He could just as easily be looking for his mom, or a brother or sister. He peered harder at the woman's face, trying to decide if she was a friend, if she was safe. Suddenly her eyes flashed at him and he staggered back. Bright green flashes that seemed to physically push him backward! That's exactly what Henry described when he was talking about the witch.

He spun on his heel and dashed back into the safety of the boy's bathroom. He slipped into an empty stall, his heart beating rapidly. What was he going to do now? He waited for a minute for his heart to calm down, and suddenly got an idea.

He glanced at the corner of his glasses where the mirror was, saw the image of his face, blinked and said "invisible" out loud. He felt a slight tingle, took a deep breath and walked out of the stall. He raised up on his toes and looked at the mirror over the sink. There was no one there. He smiled and waited for another boy to walk out of the bathroom, and followed him out of the open door. He stopped and looked around at the crowd. The woman was still there, watching the bathroom door, obviously waiting for him.

He walked to the left, skirting as far away from her as he could get as he looked for his dad. He glanced over at the woman after he passed and she had her head up, almost sniffing the air, trying to find him. He turned and almost ran into his dad, who was walking toward the bathroom. He waited for him to pass, glanced at the corner of his glasses and whispered "visible". He felt a tingle and looked down at his hands. They were there. He was visible again.

"Dad, I'm right here," he said with a small smile. His dad turned.

"There you are. It's time to go back in."

"OK," he said, reaching up and taking the hand his dad offered. Together they walked back into the theater, and he never looked back.

CHAPTER THIRTY SEVEN

Charlotte was still excited from the performance. She loved being on stage and the adrenalin was still pumping through her as she talked with the other actors in the school library, which was being used as a waiting area where students met with their parents.

A tall woman in a plain dress walked up to her and smiled as she handed Charlotte a bouquet of flowers.

"You were wonderful tonight, dear" she said.

Charlotte smiled back and took the flowers from her.

"Oh, thank you. These are very nice."

She looked more closely at the woman and realized she didn't know her.

"I'm sorry, I don't recognize you. Are you a friend of mom's?"

The woman smiled.

"Not really. I'm new here, and I was just really pleased with your performance. I thought you were wonderful. My name is Sara."

Charlotte leaned closer to the woman and tried to study her face. She looked normal, and Charlotte smiled at her.

"I'm Charlotte."

"I know."

"Hi sweetie," Charlotte's mom called out from ten feet away. Charlotte turned toward the voice and smiled.

"Hi mom."

Her mom arrived and they hugged.

"Where did you get the flowers?"

"Oh, from this person here."

Charlotte turned to introduce her mom to Sara, but she was gone.

CHAPTER THIRTY EIGHT

Everyone was gathered in the living room of the clubhouse snacking and trying to relax. But it wasn't working. The conversation kept circling back to the witch.

"She's a middle aged woman, with dark hair and wrinkles," offered Annabelle.

"Not when we saw her," replied Quinn. "She was older, but she did have dark hair. What was different were her really weird eyes."

"Her hair was long and she was very old when I saw her at the play," Garrett offered.

"So, she can make herself look however she wants to look," Charlotte jumped in. "I may have met her too. I think she's trying to get close to one of us so she can talk her way into the clubhouse."

"Can she trick one of us into letting her in?" asked Chugga. Henry nodded and answered.

"I think she thinks she can, but I'm sure CC would never let her in. But we still have to be careful. And, eventually, we are going to have to make a stand against her and make it clear she has to go away and leave us alone."

"How do we do that?" asked Annabelle.

"I don't know," Henry replied.

"How did Grandpa get rid of her?" asked Chugga.

"I don't know, but he told me he wouldn't be able to help us with this. He said we have to get rid of her ourselves."

"Great," murmured Charlotte.

It was quiet for a long time as everyone considered their plight. Finally Quinn spoke up.

"Why don't I just threaten her?"

Annabelle scoffed.

"Quinn, you have no idea what powers she might have."

"If her powers are so great, why can't she get in here? Why hasn't she just grabbed one of us and made us bring her in here?" Quinn replied.

It was quiet again until Garrett said in a very soft voice.

"She was very scary when I saw her."

"Can Grandpa at least tell us what her powers are?" asked Annabelle. Henry shook his head.

"He said he doesn't know. When he came to help me get out to come help you and Cody, she was throwing fireballs at the clubhouse wall. He said he'd never seen her do that when he was fighting her."

"Great," Charlotte said again.

"So, we need a plan," Henry pressed. "I think one of us will have to confront her in her normal state and try to find out what she wants."

"I already said I'd do that. I'm not afraid of her," Quinn stated.

Annabelle just shook her head.

"Let's see what she does the next time one of us comes in contact. Let's don't push it. Maybe we're overreacting."

Everyone nodded except Quinn, and the rest of them hoped he wasn't the one to see her next.

CHAPTER THIRTY EIGHT

The next afternoon Annabelle got off the school bus at the end of the long driveway up to the main house and her cottage. She turned to wave goodbye to her friend Stella, but Stella wasn't looking at Annabelle. Instead she was looking over Annabelle's head up the driveway. Annabelle turned around to see what Stella was looking at and saw the red and blue flashing lights behind the house.

"Oh, no," she said and began running up the road. A hundred terrible thoughts flashed through her mind as she ran, worries about the horses and mostly about her mom. By the time she reached the top of the driveway, she was out of breath and very scared.

There were three police cars parked back by the main entrance to the barn. At first Annabelle couldn't see anyone but policemen, but then she saw her mother talking to one of them and she let out a huge sigh of relief. At least her mom was OK.

She ran up to her and her mom saw her and opened her arms. Annabelle rushed into them and hugged her mom hard.

"What's happened?" Annabelle almost whispered.

"Prince Eversoul is gone," her mom replied as she hugged Annabelle and rubbed her head. Annabelle pulled away and looked at her mom. She couldn't believe it was true.

"Gone where?"

"We don't know."

"You mean, someone stole him?"

171

Her mom just shook her head and they both looked up as the head policeman approached them, adjusting his heavy belt.

"Anything?" asked her mom.

The man just shook his head.

"Not yet. No signs of forced entry because the barn doesn't even have doors in some places. And no signs of a struggle in his stall."

The policeman paused and looked at the main house.

"And you say the owner of this place is away somewhere?"

"Mister Layman is in Barbados, on holiday. He won't be back for another week or so."

The policeman wiggled his shoulders.

"I see."

Annabelle could hear the envy in the policeman's voice.

"Prince didn't just run away. Someone stole him, right?" Annabelle asked.

"That's what we are assuming," the policeman replied. "Ground's a little hard, so not much help with tire tracks."

"When did it happen?" Annabelle asked.

"We don't know. The last time I can remember seeing him was last evening when I brought the horses in for the night," answered her mom. The policeman looked at Annabelle's mom.

"You didn't hear anything, or see anything at all?" he asked.

"No. Nothing last night, and I was gone most of the day today. I was in New Jersey looking at a horse for one of my clients."

"Anyone else here?"

"Not that I know of. My helpers don't come in until later today."

"So, nobody around but the horses," he said, looking out at the field at the horses still there. "Too bad they can't talk to us."

Annabelle's head snapped up and she almost blurted out that they actually could talk, but she caught herself just in time. She glanced at the field and then at the barn, all of a sudden dying to talk to the horses. She was sure she could get some answers.

"Is it OK if I go in and make sure the other horses are OK?"

Her mom looked at the policeman and he nodded.

"Sure," he said, looking around. "We're pretty much done in there."

Annabelle nodded and raced into the barn. Maybe she could get to the bottom of this mystery quickly. At least one of the horses had to have seen something. The hardest part would be how to explain to the policeman how she learned what happened. She decided she'd figure that out later. First she had a lot of horses to interview.

CHAPTER THIRTY NINE

It wasn't going nearly as well as Annabelle had hoped. She couldn't believe it, but it seemed like none of the horses had seen anything at all. Either their stalls were in the wrong aisle, or they were asleep, or they were out in the field, or the kidnappers were just very quiet and Prince didn't put up a fight. She finished talking to Cody, her last hope, and still didn't know anything new. She didn't even know when he was taken. It could have been during the night, or in broad daylight.

She was very disappointed. She had hoped that she could learn something helpful and play a key role in getting Prince back. What good was it to be able to talk to animals if they didn't know anything when she needed them!

She walked back outside and looked around. The police were all gone and her mom was just standing and looking out at the fields. Annabelle walked over to her and snuggled up against her. Her mom put her arm around her.

"Don't worry, sweetie. They'll find him and bring him back," her mom said as she rubbed her head.

"I hope he's OK."

"I'm sure he is. If they wanted to hurt him, they wouldn't have taken him away."

"Why would anyone take him in the first place?" Annabelle asked.

"He's worth a lot of money."

"You mean they kidnapped him?" Annabelle was surprised.

"Probably."

"Maybe they just want to use him to have colts with their own horses," Annabelle guessed.

"Maybe, but then you couldn't tell anybody he was the sire, so you'd lose a lot of the value."

"Will we be in trouble for losing him?"

"No. Mister Layman has insurance on him, so he won't lose any money."

"But maybe he likes him and will be very sad that he's gone?" Annabelle said.

"I don't think so. He doesn't seem to care that much about horses."

"But, still," Annabelle said and her mom just nodded. Finally her mom took a deep breath and said "OK. I've got to feed the horses. You should go do your homework."

"Can I help with the horses first?" asked Annabelle.

"Sure," her mom replied and they both turned and slowly walked back into the barn.

CHAPTER FORTY

Everyone gathered the next day after school at CC's to talk about the missing horse.

"Do the police have any idea what happened?" Charlotte asked, clearly disturbed by the plight of the famous horse.

"Nothing at all," Annabelle replied glumly. "And I didn't learn anything by talking to the horses."

"What about all of the other animals?" Henry asked.

"What other animals?"

"Well, at the barn where I ride there are lots of other animals besides horses. Like cats, and dogs," Henry pointed out.

"And rats and mice and owls," Chugga chimed in.

"I suppose I could talk to the cat and the dog, but I don't think I am able to speak to rodents or birds," Annabelle replied.

"Why not?" asked Quinn. "Aren't they animals too?"

"Well, yes, but I think my particular gift is with mammals."

"Weird," muttered Quinn.

"I suppose I can try," offered Annabelle.

"Hey! I have an idea," offered Chugga and everyone looked at him.

"Suppose I go back to the day he disappeared and hide in the barn. Maybe I can see what happened."

"That's a great idea," Henry said. "But how will you know what time to go back to if nobody knows when the horse was taken?"

They all looked at Annabelle.

"The police don't know. It could have been anytime from about ten at night until three or so the next afternoon."

Everyone turned back to look at Chugga, who shrugged.

"I guess I can start at night and go back every half hour or so until something happens."

"Can you do that?" asked Charlotte.

"Why not. I'll go back to ten PM, and if nothing is going on, I can come back to the present and then go back to ten thirty, and so forth."

"When can you do that?" asked Annabelle, clearly excited about the possible breakthrough.

"Why not right now? You and I can walk back to the barn together and I'll start."

"Wait," Charlotte interrupted. "If you go back every half hour from ten to three the next afternoon, that's thirty four visits."

"That's a lot," chimed in Garrett.

"So, what do you think I should do?" asked Chugga.

Charlotte shrugged.

"I'd pick half way, say about seven AM the morning he was discovered missing. If he's still there, you don't have to worry about the night before. If he's gone you also have a time frame to work with. Fewer hours means fewer trips back and forth."

"Good idea," he nodded and looked at Annabelle. "Should we go now?"

"Sure," she said.

"Wait," Chugga said. "If we go now, real time will start when we go out the door here, and I won't get home for hours. Not good."

"OK. I understand. When can you do it?" Annabelle asked.

"How about tomorrow afternoon? Henry has a riding lesson right across the street. Quinn and I usually go along and we visit Grandma. But, I can say I want to come over to see you. I'll get mom to drop me off."

"What time?"

"My lesson is at five," Henry chimed in.

"That'll give us an hour for me to go back and forth. That should be enough to at least figure out when it happened."

"OK. Just come to the barn and I'll meet you there."

"Got it."

"What are you going to do if you actually see someone kidnapping the horse?" asked Quinn.

Chugga thought about it for a minute, then answered.

"I'll watch and get as much information as I can, I guess."

"Yeah," Henry agreed. "Don't try to stop them or anything, OK?"

"Hey, no problem," Chugga agreed.

They all finished their snacks and returned to their rooms to go home.

CHAPTER FORTY ONE

Chugga was right on time and Annabelle was waiting for him just outside the barn.

"OK. Let's do this," Chugga replied. "Tell me the date again that he disappeared."

Annabelle thought and told him and he punched the date and seven AM into his watch.

"Here I go. I'll be right back."

He blew on the watch and disappeared as he travelled back in time. He quickly looked into Prince Eversoul's stall. It was empty. He checked around to make sure the horse wasn't anywhere else, then hit the reset button. He reappeared and he walked over to Annabelle.

"He wasn't there, so it had to be the night before."

"OK. Let me think a minute. The last time we saw him was about seven the night before."

"My guess is, it would have been late at night that they did it," Chugga guessed.

"Agreed."

"So, maybe I'll try, like three in the morning first?"

"OK."

He reset his time machine watch and looked up at Annabelle.

"I'll be right back."

He blew on the watch and was transported back to the night in question. It was cold and dark. He walked over to Prince's stall and peered in. At first he didn't see anything in the gloom, but suddenly he saw a pair of eyes in the far corner.

"Hey!" He said and watched the eyes blink back at him. He hit the reset and returned to the present, where Annabelle was standing.

"He's still there."

Annabelle nodded.

"OK. So it happened sometime between three and seven in the morning."

"I'll try four," Chugga said and tapped in the new time. He blew on the watch and was almost stepped on by a dark shape as it passed toward the stall. He quickly slipped around the corner and slowly pushed his head back around. The shape slipped into the stall and a minute later two people emerged, one on either side of the horse.

He watched as they led the big animal out of the stall, down the aisle and out the side door, away from the big house and Annabelle's cottage. Chugga followed quietly, stopping in the shadows at the barn door. He remained there and peered out, watching the two people as they led the horse to a horse trailer parked behind the barn.

The back door was open and the ramp was down, and they easily led the horse into the trailer. One of the shapes climbed into the trailer and secured the horse. As soon as the shape came out of the trailer they secured the ramp under the trailer, closed the doors and dashed to either side of the cab of the truck pulling the trailer. They climbed in, started the engine and began to slowly pull away.

Chugga raced out and trotted up behind the trailer, trying to read the license plate. To his dismay, there was no plate on the trailer. He ran along the side and peered behind the truck, but it also had no plate. These people planned ahead, he thought to himself. He stopped and watched the truck and trailer slip down the back drive without lights.

When it reached the road it paused, turned to the right and turned on its lights. Within seconds it was out of sight. He now knew the time of the kidnapping, but nothing more. He sighed and hit the reset button, heading back to give Annabelle the bad news.

CHAPTER FORTY TWO

At the club meeting the next afternoon, Chugga filled everyone in on what he had seen. They were all as disappointed as he was.

"That's a bummer," Garrett mumbled almost to himself, but Charlotte was sitting next to him and heard it.

"I know, right?" she responded and Garrett nodded his head. "How are we going to find him?" he continued.

"Annabelle, did you try talking to the other animals yet?" Quinn asked.

"Sort of. I'm not very good at it. Talking to a cat is like speaking Spanish instead of English. But, I'm getting better at it."

"Maybe ask your star to make your power stronger," Garrett said. "It's not asking for a new power, just making the one you have bigger, or better."

Annabelle looked at him and smiled.

"Good idea."

Quinn spoke up again.

"Chugga, maybe you can go back to a time before the kidnappers get to the barn. You could hide and watch the truck come in and maybe check it out while the kidnappers are getting the horse out of the stables."

Chugga looked at Quinn like he had two heads and snorted.

"And maybe get caught and get kidnapped along with the horse?"

184

Quinn just shrugged. Henry brought the discussion back to the problem.

"How are we going to find Prince Eversoul?"

"I'll try again to talk to the other animals around the barn," volunteered Annabelle. Everyone looked at Chugga and he let out a big sigh.

"OK. I'll go back earlier and see if I can find a clue."

"Great. Anybody else have any more ideas?" Henry pushed.

Nobody did, so the meeting broke up and everyone went home.

CHAPTER FORTY THREE

Annabelle had spent an hour trying to talk to the cat that lived in the barn, the dog that lived in the main house and even a few mice she came across in the feed area, but none of them was able to shed light on the disappearance of Prince Eversoul.

She finally gave up and ended up in Cody's stall, stroking him and talking quietly.

"You know," Cody told her. "I've been thinking about that night, and I think that Prince knew the people who took him away."

Annabelle was suddenly alert.

"Why do you say that?"

"Because, he was a little startled when the people first came into his stall, but then he quickly calmed down. It was like he had been sleeping and was startled awake, but then it was like he recognized them and everything was OK."

"That's a huge help," Annabelle said, very excited about the new clue.

Suddenly a woman's voice startled her.

"Well, hello there Annabelle."

Annabelle spun around and came face to face with the witch. She was dressed in her normal brightly colored clothes and standing a little too close to Annabelle.

"Oh, hello Miss Henderson," she managed to get out.

"Talking to your horse again, are you?" she sneered.

Annabelle nodded.

"I was just telling him I was sad."

"Oh, I'm so sorry to hear that. What's the matter?"

Annabelle was torn between running away and speaking to the woman. Maybe she could learn something that might help later on.

"Well, you may not be aware of it, but a horse was stolen from the barn a few days ago."

"Why yes, I did hear about that. Such a terrible thing."

Annabelle tried not to look directly at the witch's eyes as they talked. And she stayed between the woman and Cody, who was shuffling around behind her, clearly disturbed.

"But the horse was new here, correct? It is not one you are attached to."

"Well, yes, he was new here, but I quickly get attached to any horse that boards here."

"I see. So, you have a keen interest in getting the horse back."

Something in the way she said it made Annabelle prick up her ears.

"Well, yes, of course. I don't want the poor horse to be hurt."

The witch stared at her for a moment and it felt like she could see right inside to her soul. Annabelle had to look away.

"I might be able to help you, you know."

Annabelle's head snapped back. In spite of her fear she had to ask.

"Really?"

The woman leaned closer to Annabelle and pointed her index finger at her.

"Let's discuss this," she said. Annabelle was wary, but couldn't hold down her curiosity.

"What do you have in mind?"

"Well, I didn't take the animal, of course, but I do have connections. I might be able to tell the authorities where they can find the poor thing."

Annabelle became excited in spite of herself. She almost forgot who she was talking to.

"Really? Oh, that would be splendid."

The witch stared hard at her now, and Annabelle's fear returned.

"I would want something from you in return, of course."

"Such as?" Annabelle said cautiously.

"Well, I'd love to see the inside of your clubhouse in the woods."

Annabelle knew Miss Henderson would not know about the clubhouse. Was the witch going to admit she was Miss Henderson?

"How do you know about the clubhouse?" Annabelle prodded.

The witch just raised her dark eyebrows and smiled slyly.

"What do you think?" she paused and then leaned closer. "It seems like a fair trade to me."

Just then Annabelle's mom walked into the barn.

"Hey there," she said as she walked up. "What are you two talking about?"

Miss Henderson straightened up and turned around.

"Oh, Annabelle was just telling me about the missing horse. So sad."

"Yes, it is."

"Have you heard anything from the people who took him?"

"No, we haven't."

The witch paused and turned to look hard at Annabelle.

"Well, I hope you are able to find him soon, before something terrible happens to him."

She looked at her watch.

"Oh, heavens, I've got to run. I'll be back tomorrow for my regular lesson."

With that she turned and quickly left the barn, climbed into her small black car and was gone.

CHAPTER FORTY FOUR

After the run in with Miss Henderson, Annabelle couldn't eat her dinner. Her mother asked her if she was feeling OK, and she said no. She asked if she could go to her room, and her mom agreed. Once there, she teleconnected with Henry first.

"Henry. We need to talk."

"Hey, Annabelle. What's up?"

"The witch was here earlier, in the barn."

"Are you OK?"

"Yes, but she offered to get Prince Eversoul back if I take her inside the clubhouse."

"What did you tell her?"

"I didn't tell her anything. Mom walked up just as she said it."

"Do you think she took him?"

"She said she didn't, but I don't really know what to believe."

"You can't do that, you know. Take her into the clubhouse."

"I know. What I'm worried about is what she might try next."

"We've got to figure out a way to deal with her."

"Maybe we should ask Grandpa for advice again."

"Last time he said he couldn't help. He said we'd have to deal with her ourselves."

"But maybe he has some ideas."

"OK. I'll ask him."

"Thanks."

"Sure."

"One more thing. Cody thinks Prince knew the people who kidnapped him."

"Seriously?"

"Yes. It's a great clue, but I don't know how to tell mom."

"Let me think about it."

"OK."

Annabelle took a deep breath and let it out. She felt very badly that she wasn't going to be able to help Prince Eversoul directly, but she just could not let the witch inside their clubhouse. She felt it would turn out to be a disaster if she did. They'd just have to find some other way to get Prince back, and also come up with a plan for dealing with the witch. This was not going to be easy.

CHAPTER FORTY FIVE

They had fallen into a pattern during their now regular meetings at CC's, letting Henry chair the event and lead the discussion. Today they had decided at this meeting to try to deal with two key issues. The first issue was how to go about getting the return of Prince Eversoul, and the second one was what to do in a confrontation with Hexa. Charlotte had an idea on the first subject.

"I think Annabelle should just say to her mom that she thinks maybe Prince knew the people who took him, because he would have made a fuss if he didn't know them and someone would have heard it. You know, plant the seed and maybe she'll tell the police."

"I bet the police have already checked out the people in his past. You know, like on TV when they always suspect the husband or boyfriend when a woman gets attacked?" Chugga said.

"I agree. I can't think of anything else Annabelle can say," said Henry.

Charlotte continued.

"I've also been thinking about other options, and it seems to me that our best bet is still for Chugga to go back in time and try to find out something that will help the police."

"Maybe I could do the same thing I did when someone stole your sketch book," he replied.

"You mean, go back to a time before the people came to steal him and move him somewhere else?" Annabelle guessed.

"Yeah."

Annabelle shook her head.

"I don't know where you could take him to hide him. And sooner or later he'd have to go back into his stall in our barn and the people could still come to get him then."

Henry looked at Charlotte.

"What kind of thing do you think Chugga might be able to find that would help?"

"Well, the other day I was riding in the car with my mom when she got stopped by a policeman, something about not using her turn signal. She had picked up Garrett from school and we were all going home. The policeman told her to get some papers out of the glove compartment and show them to him. I asked her later what the papers were and she said every vehicle has to have registration papers." She paused and looked around, then continued.

"Maybe Chugga could sneak into the truck that was pulling the trailer while the people are still in the stall with the horse. He could steal the papers out of the glove compartment. Then, we could pretend that we found them on the driveway near the barn. We then give them to Annabelle's mom and she gives them to the police and they use the papers to find the thieves."

"Cool," said Quinn, but Chugga wasn't as enthusiastic.

"You mean, climb into the truck? What if the people come back before I find the papers and they catch me inside?"

Quinn shrugged.

"If they see you, just time travel back to the present. No big deal."

Chugga was still not too excited about Charlotte's plan, but he realized Quinn was probably right. He could always just jump to another time. In the end, he agreed to try the idea out.

"That's super!" Henry said. "When can you do it?"

"I wish I could improve my super power so that I could not only time travel but I could pick my destination," Chugga replied.

"Maybe you can," Annabelle said. "Quinn improved his power by being able to teleport himself. All he did was say he wished he could, just like you just did."

"That's right!" Chugga said. He suddenly felt a tingle on his wrist and looked down at his watch. Next to the time and date spaces on the watch there was now a new blank field. Underneath it in tiny print was the word DESTINATION. It had worked! His wish had been granted. He smiled and showed it proudly to everyone as they gathered around.

"You can try it right now," Quinn said.

Chugga nodded, set the date and time for the time of the kidnapping, and keyed in Annabelle's barn in the destination space. He looked at the group. He was still not too excited about the possibility of being in the truck when the kidnappers returned to it. He couldn't see how that could possibly go well. But, he was committed now and there was no going back. He couldn't back out without looking like a real wimp in front of all of his cousins. So he took a deep breath.

"Well, here goes nothing."

He blew on the watch and disappeared.

CHAPTER FORTY SIX

It was darker and colder than Chugga had remembered. He was in the middle of the barn and it was very quiet. He moved to Prince Eversoul's stall and peered in. The dark shape of the huge animal loomed in the corner. He nodded to himself and worked his way to the back door. After peering around the corner to make sure the truck had not yet arrived, he slipped out and found a safe place to hide. He chose a spot behind a small out building across the dirt road that curled around the back of the barn.

He settled in to wait, and before he knew it, a truck was moving slowly down the road toward the barn. He was surprised how quiet the truck was moving, and realized that it had turned its engine off and was coasting slowly downhill. He watched it as it came to a halt right in front of him.

Within seconds both doors of the truck cabin opened and two people jumped out and moved quickly into the barn. Chugga waited until they were inside and then quickly dashed across the open area and stopped on the passenger side of the truck, keeping the truck between him and the barn. The truck was huge, much bigger than the truck his dad drove.

He reached up and tried the handle. The door was locked. He moved around to the driver's side. As he passed in front of the truck, he slipped and fell to his hands and knees. As he got up, he saw something glittering to his right on the ground. He tried to ignore it. He didn't have time for a distraction. But, for some reason, he couldn't just walk past it.

He glanced around, then bent down and picked up a piece of broken glass. At least that's what it looked like. He started to toss it away, but changed his mind. He wasn't sure why, but he felt the piece of glass was important, so he stuck the triangle shaped object into his coat pocket.

He stepped up to the driver side door and tugged on it. It was heavy but it swung open, squeaking slightly as it moved. He paused and waited to see if the sound drew any attention, but no one came out of the barn. He tugged it a little further open and managed to scramble into the cab. The dome light was not working, probably done by the kidnappers, so he was sitting in the dark. He pulled the door closed and then crawled across to the passenger side, reached forward and opened the glove compartment. It was empty.

Now what, he thought to himself. He noticed a compartment in between the two seats and popped it open. It was filled with all kinds of small items, but no paper at all. He began to worry about time. How long would it take them to bring the horse out?

He slid back across to the driver's seat and jammed his hand down into the open storage area on the driver side door. He rooted through several hard items and suddenly touched something that felt like an envelope with papers inside. He tugged it out and held it up to his face. He wasn't certain what it was, as it was too dark to read, but this had to be what he was looking for.

He heard a noise behind him and looked in the rear view mirror. The two people were leading the horse out of the barn! He slid down below the height of the seat back so they couldn't see him. He slowly slid across the center section and into the passenger side seat. He sat up and glanced into the passenger mirror, but he couldn't see anyone.

He tried to decide what to do. Should he try to open the door and slip out? Could they hear him from the trailer? He remembered the squeak when he had opened the other door earlier. His heart was pounding, or was that the horse banging against the trailer wall? He decided to go for it. He remembered the door had been locked and quickly unlocked it. He took a deep breath and put his hand on the door handle when he heard the trailer door close.

He glanced in the mirror again. One of the kidnappers was coming toward the door. It was now or never. He pushed against the door as hard as he could. It flew open and he jumped out and fell, landing on the ground just as the kidnapper reached the door. He scrambled to his feet and started to run, but the kidnapper was too fast. The person grabbed him by the arm and yanked him backward.

Chugga tried not to panic. He had to do something before the kidnapper grabbed his other arm. He had spent hours in the back yard over the last few years working on his soccer kick, and decided there was no better time than now to try it. He swung his leg as hard as he could and kicked the kidnapper in the shin.

As soon as the kidnapper let go of his arm, Chugga raised it to his face and found the RESET button on his watch. He pushed it just as the other kidnapper came around the front of the truck, and he was gone.

When he opened his eyes again, he was standing in the middle of his cousins, who were all looking at him. He tried to pretend that he hadn't been scared at all. He smiled, pulled out the envelope from his pocket and held it out to Annabelle.

"Got it," he said and they all cheered.

CHAPTER FORTY SEVEN

It turned out that acquiring the registration only solved half the problem. Next they had to decide how it should be accidentally discovered and turned over to the authorities.

"We can't just toss it on the driveway and hope someone finds it. What if a rider finds it and just throws it away?" Henry asked.

"Annabelle can just pretend that she found it and give it to her mother," Chugga offered.

"But it's been over a week since they took Prince. How do we explain the time gap?" asked Charlotte.

"We can rub it in the dirt and make it look like it's been on the ground for a week. And she just now saw it hidden under a bush or something," Quinn suggested.

"But it snowed yesterday." Annabelle objected. "Wouldn't it have gotten wet?"

"This is a lot harder than we thought it would be," Garrett added.

"I know, right?" Charlotte said. Then she had an idea. "It also snowed last week, right after they took Prince. Maybe we could say the paper was under the snow or got pushed around and ended up somewhere under a bush or something."

"Maybe we don't even have to try to explain it. It might sound too contrived. Maybe we just give it to Annabelle's mom and let the adults figure it out," Henry decided.

"OK. How about I give it to Quinn and when I'm bringing in the horses from the field tonight I connect with him and he teleports the paper to the driveway, and I find it?" Annabelle suggested.

"Great idea," Charlotte said and the all agreed. Chugga gave the envelope with the registration to Quinn and he stuck it in his pocket.

"I'll make it look a little dirty when I get it home tonight," he said.

"OK, I guess that's it," Henry said.

"Has anybody looked at the name on the registration? Maybe Annabelle knows them." Quinn suggested and pulled the envelope back out of his pocket. Annabelle nodded and opened the envelope and looked at the papers inside.

ROGER SPENSER

288 WINDING WAY

BRANDYWINE, NEW JERSEY

"Nope," Annabelle said after looking at the name. "Never heard of him. But, maybe mom has."

"OK. Let's do this," Henry said.

"Wait," Garrett said. "Weren't we going to talk about Hexa too?" They could all hear the small quiver of fear in his voice.

"Yes, we were," Charlotte agreed. "But, we're all a little tired right now. How about we save that for tomorrow, OK?"

Garrett hung his head for a moment, then slowly nodded his agreement.

"OK," he said quietly.

Everyone went to their rooms to return to their own homes, satisfied that they were close to getting Prince back where he belonged.

CHAPTER FORTY EIGHT

The plan was executed perfectly the next day. Annabelle went out with a stable worker to bring the horses in for the evening. She connected with Quinn and he delivered the envelope, properly covered with dirt on the driveway in front of them. The stable worker actually saw it first and picked it up. She stopped to open it.

"Huh. Someone lost their car registration," she said out loud. Annabelle pretended surprise. She reached out her hand.

"I can give it to mom and she'll make sure it gets back to the right person."

"OK", the girl said and handed the envelope to Annabelle.

On her way in from the barn after the chores were done, Annabelle touched her coat pocket to make sure the envelope was still there. She glanced down at the ground and stopped walking. Something shiny was wedged into the low stone wall that surrounded the area behind the back of the barn. She bent down and tugged at it. It resisted at first, but on the third tug the piece came out of the wall. It was shaped like a triangle. The sides were smooth, but she still felt that it was part of a larger object. And it felt right for her to keep it, so she placed it in her other coat pocket and continued on to her home.

She entered her house and found her mom in the kitchen.

"Hi mom."

"Hi sweetie. How was your day?"

"Good," she said and immediately held out the envelope. "Stacey found this on the road near the barn when we were coming in from the fields."

Her mom looked at the envelope and took it. She opened it and read the name. She didn't seem to recognize the name and wasn't making the connection so Annabelle finally decided to prod her along.

"I wonder if maybe it belongs to the kidnappers."

Annabelle's mom looked at her and then slowly nodded her head.

"It's a possibility," she said and looked at the name and address again.

"I don't recognize the name or the address," she said and picked up her phone. She called the police station and told them about the registration, and they agreed to send a patrolman over to pick it up. Within ten minutes the policeman arrived and knocked at the door. Annabelle's mom answered and turned over the paperwork to the policeman. He examined it carefully and looked at Annabelle's mom.

"You don't recognize the name?"

"No."

"This could be significant. Where did you find it?"

They both looked at Annabelle.

"Stacey found it tonight on the edge of the driveway near the barn when we were bringing the horses in."

The policeman nodded and put the envelope in his shirt pocket.

"OK, we'll check this out and let you know what we find. Thanks for calling us so quickly."

He looked at Annabelle.

"Tell Stacey thanks, for me, will you?"

She smiled shyly.

"Sure."

CHAPTER FORTY NINE

When Annabelle got home from school the next day there was a police car and a trailer parked in the driveway by the barn. She hurried over to find her mom and the policeman from the night before inside the barn. They were standing by Prince's stall and Annabelle shrieked with delight when she saw the big animal standing majestically inside the stall.

"He's back!" she said as she hurried inside to hug Prince. She whispered in his ear so her mom and the policeman standing outside the stall couldn't hear what she said.

"I'm so happy you're back safe. I'll come back later and you can tell me all about it, OK?"

"That's great," he replied and nuzzled her.

"And I'll tell you how we found you," Annabelle said and stepped back outside the stall. She turned and asked her mom a question.

"Where did they find him?"

"At the address on the registration. And you were right when you said he probably knew his kidnappers. They were people who had trained him several years ago."

"Why did they take him?"

"They just couldn't bear the thought that he might be so far away," the policeman replied and shook his head. "Sad, really. They are in a lot of trouble for what they did, but they did it because they love the horse so much."

Annabelle understood completely. She was dying to go back and talk to Prince about his experience. She wondered if he had been happy to see his old friends and was sad to be taken away from them again. Annabelle's mom spoke.

"I called Mister Layman and told him Prince had been recovered. He was happy to hear it. He said he was not going to keep him. He'd be too worried about it happening again. But he said to thank your friend for helping to find Prince."

She looked at Annabelle and could see she was sad.

"I'm sorry sweetie, but he'll be leaving us again soon."

"That's OK, mom. At least he'll be safe."

Annabelle was dying to tell the cousins the good news.

"I think I'll put my back pack away in the house, OK?"

She turned and headed out of the barn and toward their house, connecting as she walked.

"Hey, everyone! Prince is back. Getting the registration worked."

"Awesome," replied Quinn.

"That's really super," chimed in Charlotte. *"Is he OK?"*

"Yes, he seems fine."

"Cool."

"Thanks for all your efforts, Chugga. You saved the day!"

"Hey, no problem."

Annabelle was smiling as she entered her home. The Curious Cousins had been successful again!

CHAPTER FIFTY

Garrett was bored. He was struggling to stay awake in language arts class. He already knew how to read the book his teacher was reading to the rest of the class, and besides, he had just had lunch, which always made him a little sleepy. His eye lids were almost past the point of no return when there was a soft knock at the classroom door. He opened his eyes and sat up straight.

Miss Jenkins, his teacher, paused and walked to the door and opened it. A fifth grade student was standing there. She was probably a runner from the office, delivering a message, Garrett thought. Miss Jenkins listened and nodded and the girl stepped back into the hall. Miss Jenkins glanced around the room, her eyes coming to rest on Garrett.

"Garrett. Gather up your things and go with Miss Margo, please."

Garrett snapped fully awake. Miss Margo was probably taking him down to the main office. Normally, that wasn't a good thing, but if he was to take all of his stuff with him, something must be up. He quickly pushed all of his papers and books into his book bag. He stood and tugged the back pack onto his back and walked to the door.

"Good bye, Garrett. We'll see you tomorrow," Miss Jenkins said. Garrett waved goodbye and stepped into the hall with Miss Margo.

"Here we go," she said as she took his hand and began walking down the hall.

"Am I in trouble?" Garrett asked in a small voice.

"No, sweetie. Your mom is here to pick you up. You have a doctor's appointment."

Garrett was puzzled. Normally his mom told him at the beginning of the day about any doctor's appointments he might have.

"She didn't tell me about it this morning," he objected.

"Maybe she just forgot. At least that's what she said in the office."

"OK," Garrett said as they turned the corner and headed for the office door. He looked ahead, but couldn't really see anything clearly through the frosted glass wall of the office until they walked through the door. He spotted his mother standing at the counter talking to the secretary on the other side. The secretary glanced up and saw Garrett and waved.

"There he is!" she said and smiled at him. Garrett waved back at the woman, knowing he had seen her before but not remembering her name. His mother turned around and looked at him.

"Hi sweetie. How are you doing today?"

Garrett's eyes narrowed as he peered more closely at his mother.

"OK, I guess."

"I forgot we have a doctor's appointment at CHOP today. Sorry."

"That's OK," he said, still trying hard to study her face.

"Thank you, Margo for picking him up," she said to Miss Margo as she reached out and took his hand.

"Ready?" she asked with a smile.

Garrett didn't move and his mom bent down toward him.

"We really do have to go now," she said a little more firmly. Garrett still didn't move. When you have vision problems, all of your other senses are constantly on full alert. There was something about his mom's voice that just wasn't right. And she didn't smell the same. No matter what, his mom always smelled the same. A sweet smell. Very pleasant, not a little stinky like now. Something was wrong. His mom tugged on his arm a little impatiently. She turned her face full to him as she did so and Garrett recoiled. A pair of lizard colored green eyes had flashed at him. It was the witch!

He wanted to pull away, to run, but he couldn't. He realized that something had changed when the witch had taken his hand. It had tingled, then slowly turned numb. The tingling had moved up his arm and now his whole body was tingling. He couldn't control his body, and he couldn't even speak.

The witch turned to the secretary behind the counter and smiled.

"This is why I like to tell him ahead of time about doctor's appointments. He panics sometimes if he doesn't have time to prepare."

"Oh, it will be OK, Garrett," the woman behind the counter sympathized as the witch tugged on his arm. In spite of himself he slowly trudged along next to her. He wanted to run, to complain, to shout out, but he couldn't. He had no control over his body at all. In a few steps they were out of the office, and before he could think of anything else to do, they were out of the building.

CHAPTER FIFTY ONE

Garrett mindlessly walked along next to the witch all the way across the plaza in front of the school. They stopped next to a small black car and the witch opened the rear door and pushed Garrett into the car. She reached in and snapped a seat belt around him, closed the door and hurried around to the driver's side and climbed in.

As soon as she let go of him, control of his body began to slowly come back. He looked around for help, but there was no one near the car. He tried to open the door but it was locked. He closed his eyes and began to call for help.

"Charlotte! Charlotte. Help me."

The witch spun around and glared at him. She must have been able to read his mind, or maybe even hear his attempt to teleconnect. Either way, it was a bad thing.

"Cut it out, right now," she hissed at him and grabbed his arm. She squeezed hard and the numbness quickly returned to his body. The harder she squeezed, the weaker he felt, until his head nodded forward and he fell asleep.

Charlotte was in advanced math class when she heard Garrett calling her.

"Garrett, what's the matter?" she connected back. Garrett didn't answer, so she tried again.

"Garrett. It's Charlotte. Are you OK?"

She concentrated, waiting for a response. She was working so hard to hear Garrett that at first she didn't hear her teacher calling on her. Finally the words sank in.

"Charlotte? Are you all right?" her teacher interrupted her thoughts.

"Oh, sorry. I'm fine."

"Good. Then perhaps you can you help us with this problem?"

"What?" she replied, still trying to listen for Garrett to connect.

"The problem on the board? Can you help us with it?" her teacher pushed. Charlotte turned to the white board and stared at the equation written there. She was quickly absorbed in solving the problem and soon forgot her brother's call for help.

CHAPTER FIFTY TWO

Garrett woke up with a splitting headache. He kept his eyes screwed shut, trying to make the pain in his head go away. He remembered what his mom had told him after one of his operations and took slow, deep breaths, and waited as the pain gradually bled away. He finally opened his eyes, expecting to be in his own room at home.

He was lying on a bed, but it wasn't his bed at home. He looked around, but couldn't see anything except grey walls on all sides. There was no light except for a small lamp sitting on the floor. No furniture, no pictures on the walls, nothing. Then he remembered the witch and what she had done to him.

"Hexa," he said and shivered involuntarily. She had kidnapped him from school, and this must be a room in her house. He tried to call to Charlotte again, but something was wrong. He could hear his voice in his head saying the words, but the slight buzz and echo that usually came along with teleconnecting wasn't there. The witch must be blocking his attempt to contact with Charlotte. He tried Henry, thinking maybe a different connection might work, but got no buzzing there either. This was not good.

He sat up, wondering if the witch would already know he was awake. He got up and walked to the door and tried it, but it was locked. *Now what*, he thought to himself. He tried hard not to cry, mostly because he knew it wouldn't do any good. He had to figure out how to get out of here. He had to get home. As he looked around the room he saw the mirror attached to the edge of his glasses.

That's it! he thought. *I'll make myself invisible, and when she comes into the room, I can sneak past her and run away.* He sat back down on the bed and tried to make a plan. But, before he could really think about where he should stand when Hexa entered the room, the lock turned and the door swung open. He looked that way and cringed when Hexa walked into the room.

CHAPTER FIFTY THREE

Charlotte stayed after school to work with her gifted team on a robot they were building for a state wide competition. She was in charge of the actual construction of the robot they had designed. During the process she was rummaging around in a large cardboard box of metal parts, looking for a flat piece to use to cover the wires that controlled the robots arms when she grabbed something sharp.

"Ouch!" she said and pulled her hand out. She had a tiny puncture wound in her thumb. She leaned closer to the box and peered inside, trying to find whatever it was that had cut her. She carefully pushed pieces around until she spotted a shiny piece of what looked like a mirror in the shape of a triangle. She slowly picked it up and examined it.

"What the heck is this thing doing in a box of metal parts," she murmured. Someone must have carelessly left it there by mistake. She turned to toss it into a nearby trash can, but something made her stop. Her instinct was telling her that this piece of glass was somehow important. Although she wasn't sure why, she walked over to her back pack, opened it and placed the triangle into one of the pockets. She stared at the back pack for a moment, but she was not sure why.

She turned back to the project and quickly forgot about the glass. The group was just finishing up when there was a commotion at the door. She turned and saw her dad coming into the room.

"Hey, daddy," she said with a smile, but instantly saw the look on his face.

"What's the matter?"

Instead of answering, he walked up to her and hugged her, which was very embarrassing in front of the rest of the team. He finally pulled away.

"Let's go home, OK?"

"Sure," she said and gathered her things. She waved good bye to the team and walked out with her dad. She could tell he was upset, and suddenly Garrett's attempt to connect with her earlier in the day sprang into her head.

"Is Garrett OK?"

He was silent until they got into the car, then spoke as he started toward home.

"He was picked up at school today by someone who said she was mom."

"What? How can that be?" said Charlotte, stunned.

"A woman who looked like mom, sounded like her and knew all about Garrett picked him up, and we haven't seen him or heard from him since."

Charlotte felt absolutely awful. Poor Garrett had called for help and she hadn't followed up. She decided to try right away.

"GARRETT! I'm here. It's Charlotte. Are you OK?"

There was no answer, so she tried again.

"GARRETT. Talk to me."

Still no answer. She shifted her focus.

"Henry, can you hear me?"

She waited a moment before he replied.

"What's up?"

"Have you heard from Garrett?"

"No. Why?"

"Somebody picked him up at school today disguised as my mom."

"No way."

Suddenly the reality hit her.

"I bet it was Hexa."

"Oh, man. She's goin' down for this," Henry replied. Charlotte realized her dad was speaking.

"I gotta go. I'll get back to you later. Can you tell the others?"

"Sure."

"Sorry. What did you say, dad?"

"We didn't even know until I went to pick him up a little while ago. I don't want you to freak out, but the police are at the house."

"I'll be OK."

He fell silent and she began to think. Why didn't Garrett answer? Maybe Hexa could block their connecting. This was very bad. Hexa was obviously going all out to try to get into the clubhouse. Would she hurt Garrett to get what she wanted? She hoped not, but she'd have to get together with the cousins as soon as she could. As they pulled into their driveway she had another thought.

"Henry!"

"Yeah?"

"Tell Grandpa, OK."

"Good idea. Tell me when you know more."

OK."

Charlotte looked at the two police cars as she climbed out of her dad's car. They were here because her brother wasn't. She took a deep breath and looked at her dad.

"You OK? Are you ready for this?" he asked her.

She nodded and took his hand as they walked into the house.

CHAPTER FIFTY FOUR

Hexa stared at him with her green eyes and he cringed. He stepped back, hoping to keep her from grabbing his arm again. He looked away from her eyes and saw that she had a bag in her hand. He looked closer. It was from McDonald's.

"I brought you dinner," she said, still imitating his mom's voice.

"Don't talk like that," he said crossly without thinking.

"Don't tell me what to do," Hexa spat back at him in her normal voice and he took another step backward. She glared at him for a moment but then suddenly tried to sound friendly.

"This won't be so bad," she said. "Don't worry. All I want is to get inside the caboose. As soon as your friends let me do that, I'll take you home and everything will be fine. Sound OK to you?"

Garrett liked the sound of being able to go home soon, but he didn't want to agree with anything the witch said.

"I guess," he mumbled. Hexa nodded and stuck out her hand toward him with the McDonald's bag in it.

"Here. Be careful, there's a soda inside the bag. Don't spill it."

In spite of everything, the food smelled good and he was hungry again, so he took the bag and looked around. There was no table in the room. In fact, there wasn't anything in the room except the bed and the table lamp sitting on the floor providing a little light. He'd have to sit on the bed or on the floor. He looked back at Hexa. She was watching him. She seemed almost anxious that he would eat something.

"I have to go to the bathroom," he suddenly said.

"What?" she replied. She seemed almost surprised at the statement, as if she had no idea what he was talking about.

"You know, the bathroom? I have to use the toilet," Garrett said with as much sarcasm as he could muster. "It happens to all humans, you know, pretty much all the time."

"Oh, right," she said and turned toward the corner of the small room as if she expected a bathroom to already be there. She paused for a moment, then threw out her hand as if she was tossing something at the corner. There was a small cracking sound and a puff of smoke. When the white cloud faded away, Garrett saw a small toilet in the corner. He blinked and looked at Hexa, more afraid than before.

"Does it work?" he asked, more for something to say than to get an answer.

"Of course," she said, but still glanced at the new addition doubtfully, almost as if she didn't really know how they functioned. Garrett shrugged and put the bag on the bed. Hexa didn't move.

"I can't go with you in the room," he said.

"What?"

"You have to leave the room so I can use the toilet. It's too embarrassing."

She looked at the white porcelain object with wonder, shook her head, mumbled "whatever" and walked out of the room.

CHAPTER FIFTY FIVE

As soon as she could get away, Charlotte dashed up to her room, closed the door and slipped into her closet. Since time didn't move while they were in the clubhouse, she could go meet with the others and not miss anything in real time at home. She closed the closet door, slipped to the back of the closet, and made her way into her room at the clubhouse.

She quickly went to the living room to find everyone already there waiting for her. They all jumped up and surrounded her, hugging her and offering support.

"Hey, Charlotte," Henry said as he hugged her. Annabelle rubbed her back and Quinn and Chugga both gave quiet encouragements. Charlotte held it together until she looked past Henry and saw Grandpa looking at her. She burst into tears and everyone redoubled their efforts to calm her. Grandpa walked over and encircled her in his long arms and she buried her face in his chest and sobbed. He stroked her head for a moment and she finally regained control, stepped back and took a deep breath.

So, what do we do now?" she asked as everyone took their seats.

"We have to find Garrett and get him back," Henry said and everyone nodded in agreement.

"But, how do we do that?" Annabelle asked.

"Did anybody notice the ceiling in your room when you came here today?" Henry asked.

Everyone just stared at him, so he continued. "I just happened to look up. You know those stars that glow in the dark if you shine a light on them first?"

Annabelle and Charlotte nodded and Henry continued. "Well, there's one up there. I don't think it was there before."

Charlotte jumped up first, and everyone else quickly followed. They dashed into their rooms and quickly returned.

"Yep, There's one in my room," Chugga confirmed, and the rest agreed.

"So, that must be CC telling us we can all have another wish," Henry concluded.

"I just wish I knew he was OK," Charlotte said. Suddenly the huge flat screen on the wall behind Henry sprung to life. Everyone turned to look at it. Black and white static crackled on it for a few seconds and then a dim scene popped up. A semi-dark room with a bed along one wall and a toilet in the corner gradually came into view. Charlotte got up and walked up to the screen so she could see it better.

Suddenly she took a sharp breath.

"It's Garret."

"What?' said Chugga.

"That's Garrett sleeping on the bed," Charlotte almost shouted.

Annabelle moved closer to the screen for a better look.

"How did that happen?" she asked.

"The clubhouse must be fulfilling Charlotte's wish," Henry guessed. Suddenly Charlotte burst out with another wish.

"I wish we could."

"WAIT!" Grandpa stopped her by shouting.

Everyone looked at him, stunned to hear him shout. None of them had ever heard Grandpa shout before, and it was somewhat unnerving. He shrugged sheepishly.

"Sorry. But we have to think this through."

He looked around at all of them and continued.

"Given your recent history here, my guess is each one of you will only get one wish. We need to talk it through and decide what we want to wish for. We don't want to waste wishes."

"Why don't we just wish for Garrett to be free?" asked Chugga.

"The clubhouse probably can't do that," Grandpa answered. "If it could, he'd already be free. And maybe a wish that can't be fulfilled is still counted as a wish. Plus, even if he could be freed, Hexa could just take him back again."

"I see what you mean, Grandpa," Annabelle said. "We really have to think this through".

"You have an opportunity here. Let's don't waste it by being hasty. Charlotte used her wish, so you only have four left."

"Don't you get a wish?" asked Quinn.

Grandpa shook his head.

"I don't think so. Of course I will do everything I can to help you get Garrett back, but, like I said before, I think what she really wants is the clubhouse and you'll have to fight her for it without me."

"Bummer," mumbled Chugga.

"Yeah, it is," replied Grandpa. "The good news is, it looks like the clubhouse is going to help you fight her. And it seems to be much more powerful than all of us put together. We just have to figure out how to use its power."

They all nodded and sat back down to discuss their options.

CHAPTER FIFTY SIX

Grandpa told Henry to ask CC for a big blackboard and chalk. Henry did so and one appeared next to the giant screen they had just seen Garrett on. Grandpa picked up the chalk and walked to the board.

"OK. Let's get organized. What do we want to have happen?"

"Get Garrett home, right away," Charlotte said firmly and everyone instantly agreed. Grandpa nodded and carefully wrote *GET GARRETT HOME* in large letters on the board.

"Stop Hexa from kidnapping any of us ever again," Annabelle said, and Grandpa wrote *STOP MORE KIDNAPPINGS.*

"Figure out how to get her to leave us alone," Chugga said, and Grandpa carefully wrote *MAKE HEXA GO AWAY.*

"Can't we just kill her?" asked Quinn.

Grandpa shook his head. "I don't think so. I don't think she can die."

"Are you sure about that? Why do you think that?" asked Henry.

"She told me a long time ago, when she was trying to get me out of the caboose when it was in Indiana, that she was the one who had discovered the caboose in California in the 1890's. She said that made it hers, not mine. That would have made her at least ninety years old then, and that was almost sixty years ago."

"Did you believe her?" asked Annabelle.

"Yeah, I did."

"So, she's at least a hundred and fifty years old?" asked Chugga.

"She's at least that old. And that assumes she was, like twenty or so when she found the caboose in the first place. Who knows? She could have been much older, even then."

"Wow," said Quinn.

"So, if we can't kill her, what can we do?" asked Henry.

"Yeah. How did you get rid of her, Grandpa?" asked Quinn.

"Well, it was interesting. She tried everything to get me out of the caboose, but by using 'me too', I was too strong for her. But not strong enough to defeat her. She tried everything." Grandpa paused and visibly shivered. "She even tried snakes."

"Snakes?" Chugga said. "Why snakes?"

"Because she figured out that I hate snakes. I don't know how, but she did. So, she tried to use them to scare me away."

"You think she can figure out what you're afraid of?" asked Chugga, concern etched deeply on his face and in his voice.

"Yeah, I guess so," replied Grandpa

"What did you do?" Asked Quinn.

"I used 'me too' to pick them all up and toss them into one of the two small lakes that the caboose sat between."

"And what happened then?" asked Quinn.

"The snakes all drowned and Hexa was furious. I thought about it and realized that she had tried to scare me away, so I decided to try the same tactic. I needed to find out what she was afraid of. I had watched her reaction when 'me two' tossed the snakes into the lake, and it gave me an idea."

"What?" asked Annabelle.

"I got several buckets from my grandpa's barn and filled them with water. The next time she came by, I pretended to make a mistake and left the door to the caboose open, and hid just inside the door. As soon as she got close enough, I picked up a bucket of water and threw it on her."

"What happened?" asked Charlotte.

"Smoke began to come off her body and she screamed and ran away. So, I put buckets of water all over the place so there would always be one handy if she came back."

"Did that work?" Asked Charlotte.

"Not exactly. One day I came to the caboose and all the buckets that were outside were all frozen solid, even though it was July. I thought about it and quickly ran back to the house and got a hose out of the garage. I borrowed a pump my Grandpa had in his work room, and brought it back. I hooked the hose up to the pump and put the tube from the pump into the lake. With the pump on, I had an endless supply of water."

"Did she come back?" asked Chugga.

"Yes, and very confidently, because she knew the buckets of water were all frozen. But I lured her close to me, turned on the pump and began to hose her down. She tried to freeze the water but it was coming out too fast for her to deal with it. The wetter she got, the more she smoked, and eventually she disappeared in a puff of smoke."

"Did she come back?" asked Henry.

"Not while I was there. My grandpa died shortly after that, and, as I said before, when I went out to visit the caboose, it was gone. I assumed Hexa had somehow gotten inside and taken it away. I didn't see her again until the other day when I saw her outside of here when Henry called me."

He paused and looked around at the clubhouse and then at his grandchildren and smiled.

"Glad to see she didn't get inside. But, if she didn't take it, I still don't know where it went from Indiana or how it got here."

"Do you think the water thing will work on her now?" asked Annabelle.

"Probably not. She has probably figured out how to defeat that approach. She has probably guessed that I would tell you the story, so she must have found a way to defeat her anti-water issue. You'll have to find another way to scare her away."

He paused and looked around the room. He could see they were all a little scared. He wished he could help them more, but he knew they had to fight for the clubhouse by themselves.

"OK, enough of that. Let's get back to our list."

CHAPTER FIFTY SEVEN

"So, we've got three things so far. Get Garrett home, stop more kidnappings, and make Hexa go away. Anything else we'd like?" Grandpa prodded.

"Yeah," Henry said. "Instead of just making her go away, how can we make sure she doesn't just go away, but never comes back?"

"So, we should change number three to "KEEP HEXA AWAY".

"Good," said Annabelle.

"But, what if we wish to know how to get Garrett out and it shows us, that doesn't do us any good unless we know where he is, right?" asked Henry.

"That's good, Henry," Grandpa said and continued. "OK. Now let's be realistic. I don't see how the clubhouse can get Garrett away from Hexa. Not by itself."

Grandpa could see the disappointment showing on everyone's faces.

"But, it might be able to give us an idea on how we can do it."

This seemed to perk them up a bit, so he continued.

"In fact, it seems that the clubhouse is very smart. It might have some very good ideas on how you can accomplish all three of these things."

"So, can we make our wishes now?" asked Charlotte, clearly anxious to start the process of getting her brother back to safety.

"Well, maybe not just yet," Grandpa said. "Let's take the first one. We want to get Garrett free. If the clubhouse can't actually do that, then we've wasted a wish."

"So, what do we do?" asked Chugga.

"Maybe we should ask what we have to do to get Garrett freed. That way, if the clubhouse knows how to do it, it can show us and we can do it ourselves," suggested Henry.

"But what if it doesn't have any idea how to do it?" asked Quinn.

"Then we're no worse off. But either way, we've used a wish," Grandpa cautioned.

"So, do we do it or not?" asked Quinn.

"We've got to try," said Charlotte.

"Then, let's do it. Quinn said.

"OK. Then, lets," Grandpa said with a smile. "Annabelle, why don't you go next? You make the wish."

Annabelle paused and considered her wording. Then she had another idea.

"Wait. What if I wish that we knew where Hexa was keeping Garrett? We need to know that before we can ask how to get him free."

"Sounds good to me," Henry said.

Annabelle looked at Grandpa and he nodded. She took a deep breath and spoke in a clear and loud voice.

"I wish we knew exactly where," Annabelle started and suddenly stopped. She thought for a second and started again.

"I wish I knew exactly how to find the place where Hexa is keeping Garrett."

The room was quiet for almost thirty seconds, then suddenly the huge screen on the wall sprang to life.

CHAPTER FIFTY EIGHT

The screen jumped to life and everyone stood and moved closer for a better look. It took a few seconds for them to get their bearings, but then Henry spoke.

"That looks like Google Maps."

"I believe you are correct," confirmed Annabelle as the huge screen focused on an aerial view of the school Garrett attended.

"That's Garrett's school," Charlotte said, hope showing in her voice.

A red dot suddenly appeared on the middle of the school.

"Look!" Chugga said. The dot began to move and a hush spread over the room as everyone watched it crawling across the map. Charlotte was the most familiar with the geography around the school, so the group quietly moved to give her a clear view of the screen. She followed the red dot for several minutes until it stopped.

Henry spoke.

"Do you know where that is, Charlotte?"

"Not really. It looks like a shopping center that's near the high school."

Suddenly an address appeared at the bottom of the screen. Grandpa grabbed a pen and wrote it down. Annabelle took her phone out and entered the address.

"It is a shopping center. The address says the building is a YMCA."

"What?" Grandpa said. "Are you sure?"

"That's what it says here," Annabelle confirmed.

"Hexa is hiding Garrett in a YMCA?" Quinn asked.

"This is so weird," confirmed Chugga.

"OK. We know where he is. Now we can ask how to get him out," Grandpa said and turned to Henry. "Why don't you go next?"

Henry nodded.

"Good. We want to know how to get him out, right?"

Everyone nodded in unison and Henry continued.

"I wish I knew what we have to do to free Garrett from Hexa."

The giant flat screen went black and everyone stared at it, waiting for information. They sat for at least a minute, but nothing happened. Suddenly, a loud crash shook the room and everyone jumped. They looked in the direction of the sound, which seemed to be coming from outside the front door.

The windows along the front wall had disappeared and the wall was clearly turning cold.

"Oh, no," Henry said what everyone was thinking. "She's back."

"What?" asked Chugga.

Another crash rocked the room. Henry answered Chugga's question.

"Hexa is outside throwing fireballs at the front door again."

CHAPTER FIFTY NINE

Everyone stood and moved over to the front wall. It had turned solid, with no windows showing. Only the door remained in the wall, and the wall was already blue with ice. Charlotte turned to Grandpa.

"What do we do now?"

"I think she wants to negotiate. You know, trade Garrett for a chance to get inside here."

"So, someone will have to go out and talk to her?" Annabelle asked.

"If we open the door to go out, she can probably get in, right?" asked Chugga.

"Right. I'll go out and talk to her," Grandpa said.

"Be careful, Grandpa. You said her powers have probably gotten stronger since the last time you dealt with her," cautioned Charlotte.

"I'll go with you," Quinn said, but Grandpa shook his head.

"'*Me too*' can go out without opening the door. It'll be OK. I'll be right back."

Grandpa turned to the wall and became very still. Outside, '*me too*' stood right in front of the witch.

"What do you want, Hexa?"

Hexa spun around, looking for the source of the voice. The she suddenly recognized the voice and snarled.

"So, the young boy from Indiana is here. Interesting magic you have, throwing your voice like that."

"We want you to release Garrett, immediately."

Hexa's face scrunched up, her eyes narrowing, wrinkles appearing all over her face as she peered into the space in front of her. She raised a gnarled hand and poked a bony finger at the dead air.

"Let's discuss this, shall we?"

"I'm waiting," 'me too' replied.

Hexa waved a hand in front of her but caught only air.

"Make yourself visible, so we can talk," she insisted.

"We're talking just fine," Grandpa replied. "Release Garrett."

"First give me my caboose back."

"It's not your caboose."

Hexa's face clouded over and she threw another fireball out in front of her. It hit nothing until it crashed into the wall of ice that was once the front of the clubhouse. She seemed disappointed that she hadn't hit anything else. She continued in an ugly voice.

"It has always been mine. Your grandfather took it from me in Washington, and moved it to Indiana. When I finally found it, you were hiding in it, pretending it was yours. Now, these brats of yours are trespassing, and I want it back."

Grandpa paused, wondering how powerful the clubhouse had become. Perhaps they should let the witch inside. Perhaps the clubhouse was now strong enough to throw her out on its own. But, if it wasn't, she might be able to use the clubhouse's powers to grow her own. He shook his head. It was an awful thought. They couldn't take that risk. He needed to buy time so they could find Garrett and rescue him.

"All right. What do you propose?"

"That's better. I'm glad you're smart enough to see you can't win."

"Come on, quit gloating. How do you want to do this?"

"All you have to do is let me inside and I'll tell you where Garrett is."

"Not a chance. Bring him here. When he's safely in his own home, we'll let you in."

Hexa stared at the empty space in front of her for a long time before answering.

"It's no longer yours, is it? You're just out here talking to me because you can hide behind your little magic trick of invisibility. The children have the power now. I will deal with them."

"Not like this. They won't ever open the door to come out to talk to you."

Hexa looked at the clubhouse and nodded.

"Then, we'll have to do it someplace else."

"Fine. Pick a time and a place. They'll meet you there."

"Hmm. I'll think about it. But when I decide, you stay away. This is between me and the children."

With that she twirled her arm in the air above her head and disappeared with a loud crack and a small puff of smoke. Grandpa waited a moment to be sure she was gone before shutting *'me too'* down and returning inside.

CHAPTER SIXTY

Grandpa finally turned away from the wall and looked at the group.

"What happened?" asked Chugga.

"We talked," replied Grandpa.

"Is she going to give Garrett back to us?" asked Charlotte.

"Not right away. She figured out that you have the power over the clubhouse now, not me. She'll only negotiate with you. And she made it clear that I can't be there."

"So, what's going to happen next?" asked Quinn.

"She's going to pick a neutral place and she wants someone from the group to meet her there."

"I should go." Charlotte volunteered, visibly shaking. "He's my brother." Quinn saw her fear and stepped forward.

"I'll go with you. She doesn't scare me."

"There's a big surprise," replied Annabelle.

"So, we could wish to find out how to get Garrett out, and the rest of us could go free him while Charlotte and Quinn meet with Hexa," Chugga suggested.

"Sounds OK to me. Is that OK with the rest of you?" Henry asked.

"Maybe we should wait and see how we're supposed to get Garrett out," Quinn said.

"Why?" asked Annabelle.

Quinn shrugged.

"We each have a superpower, and we should figure out which of the powers is best for rescuing Garrett."

"Good thinking," replied Charlotte. They all looked back at the screen, waiting for it to respond to Henry's earlier wish regarding freegan Garrett.

Suddenly the flat screen popped to life. Stars floated across the huge screen, sort of like a screen saver on a computer. Then the screen went black for a few seconds and then a building appeared.

"I think that's the YMCA," Charlotte said as she moved closer to the screen. The picture moved and the building got smaller and revealed the front of the building where the YMCA sign appeared.

"That's it!" Quinn said.

The view moved around to the back of the building and zoomed in on the delivery entrance, where a huge garage door sat. The view continued to move in until a touch pad on the wall became visible. As they watched, numbers on the pad moved in and out as if being punched. The camera then zoomed back to show the door opening.

"Did anyone get the combination?" asked Grandpa.

Annabelle and Charlotte responded in unison.

"Yes."

"Good", Henry said as they all continued to watch the screen. The view moved through the door and turned left.

"This is like a video game," Quinn said. There were two more turns and the view stopped in front of a door. This one also had a combination, which was again punched in on the screen.

Henry looked at Charlotte and she waved her hand.

"Got it."

The door opened and the view went down a flight of stairs, turned right and ended in a huge room filled with stream pipes and large machines. It moved to yet another door at the far end of the room. This one had a padlock on it. They all watched, waiting for the door to be opened, but after fifteen seconds focused on the door, the screen slowly faded to black.

"So, how are we supposed to get in?" asked Charlotte.

"We break the lock," Quinn replied.

"But how?" Charlotte continued.

Everyone was quiet until Quinn spoke up again.

"We use our superpowers," he said and began to lay out a plan.

CHAPTER SIXTY ONE

Suddenly Charlotte's cell phone began to ring. She jumped in surprise and everyone turned to look at her. It was the first time any of them had received a call in the clubhouse since the time Annabelle's dad had called. Charlotte tugged the phone out of her pocket and looked at the caller ID.

The word **HEXA** floated in odd type on the screen.

"It's the witch," Charlotte stammered, stunned to see the name on her screen.

"I guess you'd better answer it," Henry replied.

Charlotte nodded and punched the answer button and put the phone up to her ear.

"Hello."

"Look at me, dearie," a scratchy voice crept out of the cell phone. Charlotte looked around the room and then realized the voice wanted her to look at the screen on her phone. She slowly pulled the phone away from her ear and held it out in front of her. She peered at the screen, which showed a swirling grey cloud. As she continued to stare at the small screen, the cloud morphed into a dark, brooding face.

"That's better," the face said, and cackled. "Now, pay attention, dearie. Tomorrow morning at exactly ten o'clock, I will be outside the clubhouse door with your precious little brother. You will open the door and let me into the clubhouse, or I'll turn your brother into a rat. Do you understand me?"

Charlotte tried to answer, but couldn't get any sound to come out of her mouth.

"Just nod your head, dearie."

Charlotte nodded and the ugly face cackled again.

"Wonderful," Hexa replied, but suddenly her face grew stern.

"Everyone says you're very smart. But don't think you can outwit me. It could cost you a brother. And don't tell your parents about this, and don't tell the police either. Mortals can't help you with this problem, dearie."

"Wait," Charlotte said, regaining her composure. "How do I know Garrett is still safe?"

"You don't. But you'll see for yourself tomorrow at ten."

"What if I'm late? It's sometimes hard for me to get away. Especially now with my parents so uptight and the police around all the time."

"Just be there tomorrow at ten. I'm sure you'll find a way."

The screen suddenly went blank. Charlotte looked at the group.

"Did you hear that?"

"Hear it? It was on the big screen," replied Chugga, pointing at the now blank flat screen.

Everyone was quiet for a moment, then Quinn spoke.

"Looks like we've got till tomorrow morning at ten to rescue Garrett."

CHAPTER SIXTY TWO

Garrett heard the lock on the door rattle and he jumped off the bed and moved to the corner of the small room. He closed his eyes and made himself invisible. He stood as still as he could as the door opened and the witch walked in. She closed the door and looked around the room.

"Well, well, well. The little one has a special skill," she said as she walked around the room. She stopped walking and called out.

"Come out, come out wherever you are."

Garrett continued to stand still and tried to control his breathing. The witch slowly turned around, her piercing eyes and oversized ears working hard to find her prey.

"All right. We'll play this a different way." She raised her arm and spun around in a complete circle, a green dust suddenly falling from the ceiling and completely covering the room. Garrett tried his best not to breathe the dust filled air, but eventually he had to take a breath. He immediately began to cough and the witch turned toward the sound.

She raised her hand again and the green dust became so thick Garrett could hardly see.

"There you are," she said as the dust settled on Garrett's body, showing him as a green shape in the corner of the room. The witch walked up to him and stopped a step away.

"You were a naughty boy, trying to hide from me. But it is a very nice power to have, being able to become invisible. Your grandfather seems to have the power too. Do all of your cousins have the same ability?"

Garrett pressed his lips together, determined to not give the witch any helpful information. His skin was burning and he had to try very hard not to cry.

"All right. You don't have to talk to me. I'll find out enough when I meet with them tomorrow. I only told your sister to meet me, but I'm sure they will all be there. If they are smart, they will let me into the clubhouse, and you will be able to go home."

She turned away and walked toward the door. She opened it and paused.

"As punishment for your little trick, I think I'll not bring dinner tonight. You look like a strong, healthy child. You'll survive it. Good night."

She waved her hand in the direction of the lamp in the far corner and it went out. She stepped out of the room and closed the door, leaving the room in complete darkness.

Garrett slowly moved back to the bed and climbed onto it. He lay down and began to cry.

CHAPTER SIXTY THREE

It had been decided that all five cousins participating in the rescue operation would be overkill and might bring too much attention to their effort. At the same time, everyone wanted to be in on it, so the discussion went on for some time. In the end, it was decided that only Henry, Quinn and Charlotte would go. Henry because he could help if Garrett was injured, Quinn because his superpower was best equipped to do battle with the witch if she was there, and Charlotte because she was Garrett's sister, and her superpower could come very well come in handy in getting the last door open.

It was Saturday morning, and the only way the members of the rescue team could easily get out of their respective houses was to have Grandpa say he was taking them out to breakfast. He picked each one up at their homes early in the morning, and they arrived at the parking lot in front of the YMCA at seven thirty. Grandpa parked a good distance away from the YMCA and cut the engine.

He turned around and looked at the cousins. Henry seemed calm, Charlotte looked nervous and Quinn had his game face on.

"OK. Does everyone know their role?" Grandpa asked.

All three nodded.

"Don't forget, we can all talk to each other by teleconnecting if we have to. And, if the witch is there, let Quinn and I deal with her, OK?"

They all nodded.

"Good. Let's go get Garrett."

Grandpa started the car again and drove across the parking lot and around to the rear of the YMCA. The building was open, but there was no activity at the rear of the building. Grandpa parked and they all got out and walked to the service entrance. Quinn and Henry watched as Charlotte recited the code and Grandpa punched it in. The door opened and they moved inside and closed it behind them.

They waited for their eyes to adjust to the low lighting, then moved across the open space to the second door. Grandpa again punched in the code that Charlotte recited and they moved inside and quickly went down the hallway. As they turned a corner Grandpa suddenly held up his hand. They all stopped and watched as a custodian slowly walked down the hall in front of them. They held their breath, hoping that he wouldn't turn around and see them.

Finally he turned a corner and they waited a moment more to be sure he wasn't coming back, then started quietly down the corridor. They stopped again when they reached the corner and Quinn peeked around to check on the custodian. He was nowhere in sight, so they moved on.

They went down the stairs and eventually reached the door that the clubhouse had indicated opened into Garrett's room. They all halted, as planned, so Grandpa could check to see if it was safe to go inside. He sent '*me two*' into the room, then quickly brought him back out.

"Who has the flashlight?"

Henry pulled it out from his jacket pocket. Grandpa took it and handed it to Quinn.

"Can you teleport this to the other side of this door? I can't take it in with me and it's totally dark in there."

Quinn just nodded, closed his eyes and a second later the flashlight disappeared. Grandpa patted him on the shoulder.

"Good job," he said and sent 'me too' back into the room. He returned in only a few seconds.

"He's in there, on a bed, and he's alone. No sign of the witch. It's dark. He didn't open his eyes when I flashed the light on him. He looks a little funny," he said and then wished he hadn't as Charlotte gasped.

Grandpa handed the flashlight back to Henry, who nodded. "Let's get him out before the witch comes to get him for the meeting."

Quinn was checking the padlock.

"It looks pretty strong," he said. They had discussed the idea of bringing a crowbar or bolt cutters with them to deal with the pad lock and decided that it would not look good if they were seen or stopped inside the building carrying either of those items. Instead, they had decided to let Charlotte use her superpower.

Quinn was already pulling a short but very sturdy chain out of his pocket. He slipped it through the locking mechanism and turned to Charlotte.

"Ready?"

Charlotte nodded. Everyone moved away from her as she prepared to change. She closed her eyes, muttered a few words and everything around her shimmered for a moment, and then cleared. When they could all see again, they were stunned to find a fully grown gorilla standing there, even though it was what they had planned. Quinn held out the two ends of the chain and the gorilla took it in its hands. The gorilla filled most of the space in front of the door and the others moved further away from it to give it room to maneuver.

When Henry nodded at the gorilla, it stepped backward and tugged on the chain. With its remarkable strength, the gorilla easily ripped the padlock away from the door. Quinn stepped forward and pulled the door open. Henry turned the flashlight on and pointed the light into the room. He and Quinn stepped in while Grandpa stayed out in the hall to act as a guard. The room was small and it was easy to find the bed. Garrett was sitting on the bed, blinking his eyes at the light.

Charlotte had quickly turned back to herself and now dashed into the room. She pushed past Henry and threw her arms around Garrett. They both started crying as they hugged each other. Charlotte finally pushed Garrett away from her so she could see him better.

"Are you OK?"

"Better now," Garrett sniffed.

"Why are you all green?" Quinn asked.

"The witch did it to me when I was invisible. It still hurts."

Henry stepped over.

"Here, let me fix it for you."

He hugged Garrett and whispered to him. Garrett changed back to normal and sat down on the bed and they all watched as Henry turned green for a moment.

"That was interesting," Charlotte said as Henry slowly turned back to his normal color.

"Garrett was right," Henry said as he shook his head. "It does hurt."

"Uh, guys, can we get going?" Quinn said and Henry agreed.

"He's right. Let's get out of here."

Charlotte almost lifted Garrett off the bed and put him on his feet on the floor. She took his hand and they all started for the door. They stepped out into the hallway and Garrett saw Grandpa.

"Hi, Grandpa," he said in a wavering voice.

"Hi, buddy."

"Whew. It stinks out here," Garrett said. "It smells like a zoo."

Everyone laughed and Grandpa began herding them all back down the hall, pausing at each turn to make sure the coast was clear. Within minutes they were out of the building, where they crossed the parking lot and began piling into Grandpa's Jeep. Quinn stumbled slightly and had to put a hand down on the ground to keep from falling. His hand touched something warm and he looked down to see a shiny triangular shaped piece of metal. Without thinking he scooped it up and jammed it into his pocket.

He jumped into the Jeep just as Grandpa started it up and pulled back out to the public parking area, where he paused for a moment while everyone took turns hugging Garrett. Finally Grandpa spoke.

"OK, Garrett. We have to talk."

CHAPTER SIXTY FOUR

Grandpa smiled at Garrett and tasseled his hair.

"Are you OK?"

"Yeah. Pretty much."

"Good. We're going to take you home now, OK? Your mom and dad are going to be very excited to see you. There will also be policemen there and they will ask you a lot of questions."

"About the witch?"

"Yes, and how she took you and where she kept you. Just answer their questions as best you can, OK?"

"OK."

"They aren't going to believe you about the person being a witch," Charlotte inserted.

"But it was the witch," Garrett insisted.

"I know. But grown-ups don't believe in witches."

"Grandpa does."

Grandpa laughed.

"Yes, I do, buddy. But a lot of other grown-ups don't believe I'm a grown up yet."

Garrett smiled.

"You're silly, Grandpa."

Grandpa nodded and looked at the rest of the group.

"Everybody else know the story?"

They all nodded and Charlotte started.

"We can't lie to our parents, so we take pieces of what happened and tell them. A woman called me and said she had Garrett and we could have him back today. She said she's meet me in the woods behind Annabelle's house. She said she wanted to be part of our club, to be able to come into our clubhouse. She said I couldn't tell my parents or the police."

"Don't forget the part about how you knew he was in the YMCA," added Henry.

"Oh, yeah. While she was talking I had this, like vision of the YMCA near our house. It was just like it was on a giant TV screen right in front of me," Charlotte said with a smile.

"And you asked me and Quinn to come along because I'm the oldest and Quinn is the toughest," added Henry.

"Right. Then I called Grandpa and told him everything and he said he'd help us."

"Good. You'll do just fine," Grandpa said with a soothing smile.

"But I bet the grown-ups and the police are going to be mad at you for doing all of this without telling them," Quinn said and Grandpa nodded seriously.

"I know. But that's OK. I can handle them. Lots of people have been mad at me before. I'm pretty much used to it."

"Better you than me," Quinn said.

Grandpa put the Jeep in gear.

"OK. Let's do this. Charlotte, call your mom and tell her we found Garrett and we'll be home in ten minutes."

Grandpa hit the gas and they headed for home. As he passed the YMCA building he glanced at the service entrance and saw a vaguely familiar shape slip through the door.

CHAPTER SIXTY FIVE

Everything went pretty much as they expected when they reached Charlotte's house. Her parents were ecstatic to see Garrett, and the police asked dozens of questions. No one believed a word about a witch being involved and everyone was furious with Grandpa for not telling anyone what he was up to and especially for taking the children along while he was doing it.

But Grandpa weathered the storm pretty well, and eventually he was allowed to take Henry and Quinn home while the police went to the YMCA and Charlotte's parents took Garrett to the hospital for what they called precautionary testing. They wanted to make sure he didn't have any hidden injuries. As Grandpa drove them home, Henry and Quinn teleconnected with Chugga and Annabelle, spreading the good news and all of the details about Garrett's rescue.

It was hours later when the Wise family returned from the hospital, Garrett receiving a clean bill of health. He and Charlotte both asked if they could go to their rooms to rest and the parents willingly agreed. Five minutes later everyone was gathered in the clubhouse living room, celebrating by drinking Coca Cola, apple juice or lemonade, and eating from the dining table.

"Did Hexa really make a toilet appear out of nowhere?" Chugga asked Garrett.

"Yes, and it worked too."

"And when you were invisible she found you by spreading green fog around the room?" asked Annabelle.

Garrett nodded and smiled.

"It smelled pretty bad." Garrett said, "But not as bad as the hallway smelled when you rescued me."

Everyone had been part of the plan for Charlotte turning into a gorilla in order to have enough strength to break open the pad lock, and they laughed about it now. Garrett was confused, so Charlotte told him what she had done.

"Very cool," he said and smiled. "I wish I could have seen that."

"Yeah," said Quinn. "What was it like being a gorilla?"

"It felt kind of weird."

"I'm quite certain it did," Annabelle said with distain.

"I bet the witch is really going to be mad at us now," Garrett said.

"No doubt," replied Annabelle and the rest of the group nodded in agreement. Just as he said it, Charlotte's phone buzzed. She looked at it and saw the same milky clouds on the screen as the last time Hexa had called her.

"Oh, no. Here we go again," Charlotte groaned. She pushed the power button to turn the phone off, but the milky clouds didn't go away.

"You can't get rid of me that easily, dearie," the scratchy voice said. "I don't know how you found him, but you'll all pay for it. You can count on it."

With that the screen went blank and Charlotte stuffed the phone back into her pocket.

"How does she do that?" Charlotte asked no one in particular.

Henry shrugged. "She has a lot more than one superpower."

"Seriously," Chugga said

"We need a plan, like, now. We can't wait for her to do something else to us," Henry said and they all nodded.

"Who still has a wish left?" Annabelle asked, and several raised their hands.

"Good. So why don't wish we knew how to get rid of the witch?"

"I think we have to be careful what we ask," Charlotte said. "We want to make her go away and leave us alone forever. Right?"

"Why don't we just ask how to kill her?" Quinn asked.

"Grandpa said he didn't think we can kill her," Chugga replied.

"I think the way Charlotte just said it is good," Henry said.

"OK. Let's do it," Quinn said, clearly impatient. "Whose turn is it to wish?"

"I'll go," Chugga said.

"Wait," Annabelle said. "We have to make sure we describe what we want so the clubhouse clearly understands our wishes."

"So, I should wish that we knew what we had to do to get rid of the witch?" Chugga asked.

"Maybe not get rid of her. Maybe that's not clear enough," Charlotte chimed in.

"Yeah," Henry added. "Maybe how do we make sure she goes away and never comes back to bother us again?"

"That sounds better," Annabelle approved.

"OK. So, you got that, Chugga?"

"I think so," he said and took a deep breath and turned toward the black screen as if it was what he was talking to.

"I wish we knew how to make the witch go away and never bother us again," he declared in as solemn a voce as he could muster. Everyone's head snapped around to look at the giant screen with him, waiting for an answer. The screen remained dark for ten seconds, and then ten more, and then ten more. Finally Chugga broke the tension.

"What'd I do wrong?"

No one could give him and answer, so they all remained silent.

CHAPTER SIXTY SIX

As they all sat, silently trying to figure out what the problem might be, the screen suddenly sprang to life, filled with a murky, swirling mass of iridescent colors moving across the screen, not unlike the aurora borealis. Everyone stared, mesmerized by the colors and their movements. Finally Quinn spoke their thoughts out loud.

"Anybody have any idea what that is?"

"What is CC trying to tell us?" asked Charlotte.

"It's thinking," offered Garrett and the screen suddenly brightened for a moment then returned to its normal colors.

"I think you're right, Garrett," Henry said and Garrett grinned at the praise. The screen then slowly changed from the bright colors to a large star that dominated the entire screen.

"It's another star," Chugga said. "Like the ones we wished on to get our powers."

As they watched the star separated into five triangles and the center piece that held them all together.

No one said anything as the star came together again, then separated into six pieces, and then came together again.

"Any idea at all what it's trying to tell us?" asked Henry.

"Well, there are six pieces, and there are six of us," Annabelle suggested. As she said it the screen brightened for a moment.

"That means yes," Chugga said.

"And maybe the way it comes together means the six of us have to work together to defeat the witch," Charlotte added, and the screen brightened again.

"But what is it we're supposed to do together?" asked Chugga.

The screen suddenly became dull, then the star split apart, then each of the five triangles that made up the five points of the star flashed brighter in turn, then the center piece flashed, and finally they all came back together and the star they formed flashed. Then the screen went blank.

"Wow, that's the clue?" asked Quinn.

"I guess we'll have to think about it and figure it out," Chugga said and they all nodded.

"Don't worry, I'll figure it out," Garrett said and they all laughed and he smiled and continued.

"But right now I want to go home."

They all nodded and agreed to work on the problem and meet again the next day. They got up and went to their own rooms to get back home.

CHAPTER SIXTY SEVEN

Things weren't much better the next day when they all gathered to discuss the problem. When they had all selected a snack from the food table Henry started them off with a question.

"Anybody come up with a solution to the mystery video?"

The all shook their heads and sat in silence. Quinn finally broke the spell.

"You know, it's a very nice day outside. I wish there was a picnic table outside under a shade tree, so we could all sit there and eat and talk. Maybe we'd get some better ideas."

Chugga went to the door and opened it. He turned to the group.

"Good idea, Quinn. Looks like CC's now has outdoor seating."

They all moved quickly to the door and looked out. There, to the left of the door, was a large picnic table laden with snacks and drinks, all protected by a giant oak tree.

"That tree wasn't there before," Annabelle pointed out.

"Who cares," said Garrett and dashed out and sat down at the table. Everyone else followed and they all quickly became engrossed in picking out their favorite snacks and drinks and chattering aimlessly in the balmy breeze under the shade tree. Fifteen minutes passed before Charlotte guided the conversation around to their problem.

"So, what are we going to do about our problem with Hexa?" she said as she munched on a perfectly grilled cheese sandwich. They all jumped as a voice came from the edge of the clearing.

"Yes, what are you going to do about me?"

They all turned toward the gravelly voice. To their collective horror, Hexa was standing in the clearing in her black robes and hood. Her green eyes were shining out of the darkness inside the hood. They collectively glanced at the caboose and saw the front closed with ice forming on it. Henry, Chugga and Quinn instantly jumped up and put themselves between Hexa and the others.

"Oh, what a gallant demonstration. I'm touched," Hexa growled at them.

"Do you really think you can protect anyone from me?" she continued.

As they stood there in defiance, she turned to the side, reached back with one arm and a fire ball appeared. She hurled it toward the edge of the clearing and it flew toward the trees. It crashed into one and the tree instantly began to burn brightly. She turned back to face the three boys.

"Would anyone like to play some catch?" she asked and cackled with a wicked voice.

"You'll burn down the woods," Annabelle said from the table. "Not a good idea. The fire company will have to come out here."

Hexa studied her for a moment, then flicked her hand toward the burning tree and the fire was instantly put out.

The three boys tried to remain brave and calm, but this was clearly a mismatch they couldn't win. Suddenly Quinn got an idea. He turned and whispered to his two brothers.

"Listen, you two get behind me. Let me handle this."

"Quinn, don't do anything stupid, OK?" Henry pleaded. Quinn just glanced at him and Henry saw the hardness in his face.

"OK. We'll be right behind you," Henry said as he stepped back and pulled Chugga with him. Quinn turned back to face Hexa.

"OK, witch. Show me what you've got."

Hexa was surprised.

"Well, quite the brave little man, are we? Do you really think your feeble powers, whatever they are, will protect you from me?"

"Why not try it and see? I'll be glad to play catch with you."

"Wouldn't it be easier, and certainly safer for you all, if you just let me into the caboose? You should never have let yourself all be caught outside its protective walls, you know."

Henry glanced back at the clubhouse. The wall was still closed up and ice was growing.

"It's still closed," he whispered to Quinn, who just stood his ground and glared at the witch.

"You don't scare me. Nobody scares me," Quinn growled at Hexa.

"Then you're not as smart as you think you are, young man."

"Quinn, you don't have to do this," Annabelle called out, but Quinn stood his ground.

"So, give me your best shot. Toss one of those fire balls at me," he said to Hexa.

Hexa studied Quinn for a moment, then finally nodded.

"Very well. But not just one. Let's see if you can handle two at once."

"Bring it on, old woman."

Hexa's green eyes flashed at the insult and she drew her arms back and the fireballs appeared in her hands. She paused, perhaps to take careful aim, and then threw them both forward. The two blazing fireballs flew toward Quinn at remarkable speed. He stood stock still, then raised his hands as if he was going to catch the fire balls.

When they reached him he muttered to himself and the fire balls touched his hands and disappeared, then exploded against Hexa's face. As soon as they had touched his hands he had teleported the fire balls back at Hexa. Her hood and robes burst into flames and she shrieked and stepped backward. She waved her hands and the flames instantly disappeared, but her robe and hood still smoked and smoldered. She glared at Quinn.

"So, the young one is more formidable than I thought," she growled as she glared at him. Quinn just smiled at her and turned around. He sauntered to the picnic table, taunting her. He stopped at the table and looked at the contents.

"I wish we had some watermelons. Really big ones," he said. He glanced back at Hexa and then turned back to the table, where a half dozen large watermelons had appeared. He smiled, nodded and picked up the biggest one.

"Let's see how good you are, old woman," he said. The watermelon disappeared and suddenly exploded against Hexa's robes. Quinn picked up another and another, teleporting each one against different body parts as fast as he could grab them up. They exploded against her in a brilliant display of red with black seeds until finally Hexa shrieked and disappeared in a puff of smoke.

"That was awesome," Garrett said as he jumped down from the picnic table and ran to Quinn. "You scared her away."

Quinn shrugged.

"She's gone now, but she'll be back."

"Didn't it hurt when you touched the fire balls?" Annabelle asked. Quinn looked down at his hands. They were red and blistered.

"Yeah, they do hurt a little," he said in an understatement.

"Here, let me fix those," Henry said and took Quinn's hands into his. He whispered his special words and the hands instantly healed.

"Wow, that's hot," Henry said, shaking his hands as he briefly experienced the pain he had taken from Quinn.

"Thanks, Henry," Quinn said.

"No problem," Henry replied. "But, we obviously still have a problem. A big one. We've got figure out the message we were given. You can't duel it out with Hexa every time she catches us outside CC's."

"I agree. And besides, she may have more powers she hasn't shown us yet," Charlotte said.

They all agreed and reluctantly went back inside to discuss their problem.

CHAPTER SIXTY EIGHT

Things didn't improve once they were inside the clubhouse. No one had any idea how they were going to deal with Hexa.

"Maybe we should just let her inside once. Maybe CC can deal with her on its own," suggested Chugga. Suddenly the flat screen on the wall burst into bright primal colors that swirled angrily around.

"Well, clearly that's not an option," Annabelle said, interpreting the display as a vigorous no to Chugga's suggestion.

"Sorry, CC," Chugga said quietly and the colors changed to soft pastels.

Suddenly Garrett spoke.

"Hey, it's like we're all talking with CC right now."

Everyone looked at Garrett and Chugga smiled.

"I think you're exactly right, buddy. CC seems to be talking back to us."

"So maybe we can ask direct questions instead of trying to figure out how to word our wishes," Quinn said.

"Are we seriously considering carrying on a conversation with a train car?" Charlotte asked, shaking her head. "It's an inanimate object. It's not like it's a living person."

When she said it the flat screen burst into violent dark colors that swirled around angrily.

"Maybe you should apologize to CC, Charlotte," Henry said quietly.

Charlotte rolled her eyes but nodded.

"OK," she said softly, then spoke louder. "I'm sorry, CC. It's just a little hard for me to comprehend that we can communicate directly with you. But, I'm trying to get with the program."

She looked at Henry and shrugged, but it seemed to work because the colors on the screen changed to soft pastels that floated gently across the screen. Chugga tried next.

"So, CC, can you tell us how to get rid of Hexa?"

The soft pastels continued to float around and Quinn jumped in.

"I can't beat her by just teleporting her fireballs back at her, can I?"

The colors grew darker and Charlotte kept up the probing.

"We think you were trying to tell us before that it will take all of us working together. Is that right?"

The colors softened again and Chugga continued.

"We get that, but we don't know what we're supposed to do."

The screen changed and began to run the same scene it had shown the night before, a star slowly rotating, its points shining.

"We get that, all together," Quinn said, slightly irritated. "But what are we supposed to do all together?"

The star spun a little faster and the five points split into five triangles and separated from the center base. An initial appeared in each triangle, corresponding to the initials of the group.

"There's only five stars, and six of us," Chugga pointed out, and the screen quickly focused in on the center base the triangles had all been attached to. It showed the initial 'G' on it.

"Oh, I get it. The sixth part is the center piece," Quinn said. The screen flashed brightly and then went blank. They all stared at it for a moment, and when it no longer came back to life they looked at each other.

"Anybody got any ideas?" Chugga asked. No one spoke for some time as they all wrestled with the problem.

"We're no further along than we were when we started," complained Chugga.

"We've got to figure this star clue out," Annabelle stated.

"And soon," Chugga added.

"OK. Everybody think about it and let's meet again tomorrow."

They all agreed and slipped into their own rooms and went home.

THE INCREDIBLE COUSINS AND THE MAGIC CABOOSE

CHAPTER SIXTY NINE

Charlotte was working on her computer, doing Japanese cartoon art drawings called Anime and placing them into short videos. She finished one, posted it on the internet and stood to take a break. She walked over to the large bird cage that housed their pet cockatiel, Mako and peered inside. Mako was sitting on a perch looking at herself in a small mirror.

"Stop primping," Charlotte teased and opened the door to the cage. She reached in and put her hand next to Mako, who quickly jumped onto the offered hand. As Charlotte started to slowly draw her hand out her eyes fell on the triangular shaped piece of glass she had found a few days earlier and placed in the cage for Mako to enjoy.

She had a sudden flash of comprehension and slowly placed Mako back on her perch.

"Oh, my gosh," she said out loud as she absent-mindedly closed the door to the cage. She stepped back and began teleconnecting with her cousins.

"Henry! Are you still up?" She wasn't sure how to teleconnect quietly. She knew Henry liked to sleep. What teen age boy didn't? So she let out a sigh of relief when he answered.

"Yes."

"I think I've figured out the video CC has been showing us."

"Really? How?"

She started to tell him about taking Mako out of the cage, but decided to skip the details and cut to the chase.

"I know what the triangles are. At least I think I do."

"What?"

"Have you found any pieces of glass lying around recently?

There was a pause as Henry thought about the question for a moment, then replied.

"Actually, I did, when I was helping Annabelle with Cody. And it's shaped like the triangles in the video."

Charlotte felt a chill of excitement run through her. She had been right.

"My guess is all of us have found one. And when we put them together, we'll have the thing that CC has been showing us. And, hopefully it will tell us what to do next."

"Awesome. I'll spread the word. Let's meet tomorrow morning at CC's at eight and see what happens when we put them all together."

We can't do eight. School. And Annabelle gets on the bus at seven."

"Oh, right. OK. After school. About four?"

"Can't. I have advanced...."

Henry interrupted her. At the moment he didn't want to hear what skill Charlotte was advanced in, unless it was witch fighting.

"OK. When then?"

"How about five?"

"OK."

"See you then."

"Charlotte?"

"Yeah?"

"Good job."

"Thanks Henry."

CHAPTER SEVENTY

The next morning Charlotte was finishing her breakfast when her mother hurried into the kitchen.

"Hi, honey," she said and kissed Charlotte on the top of her head.

"Hi, mom."

"Listen. I have an early meeting today so I have to leave right now. Can you walk Garrett to school?"

"Sure."

"Thanks. Got to run. See you tonight. Love you lots."

"Love you too, mom."

In a flash her mother was gone. Her dad was a teacher at the high school, so he had already been gone for over an hour, leaving Charlotte alone with Garrett, who now stumbled into the kitchen.

"You're late. Better eat fast. We have to leave in five minutes."

"OK," Garrett mumbled and began spooning cereal into his mouth. Five minutes later they were on their way to school. It was an easy walk, only about ten blocks with only one turn at the light at the end of the street. They were walking together and not talking much for the first three blocks when a shadow passed across their path. Charlotte looked up and stopped cold, grabbing Garrett by the arm. Hexa was standing right in front of them.

"Well, well, well. What have we got here?" She cackled. "The two Wise children on their way to school."

Charlotte instantly grabbed Garrett by the shoulders and pushed him behind her. She then calmly teleconnected with him.

"Garrett, make yourself invisible and hide behind that tree on the right. Stay there until I get rid of her."

Hexa heard her and almost shouted at Charlotte.

"Stop that, right now."

Charlotte ignored her and connected with Garrett again.

"Did you hear me?"

"Yes. But I'm scared."

"Me too. Just do it. Now!"

Garrett did as he was told and Hexa instantly saw it.

"So, the little one is going to try to hide from me, is he? Very well. I'll find him after I deal with you," Hexa said, glaring at Charlotte. Charlotte was frantically rushing through every animal she could think of, trying to come up with one who could stand up to the witch. She was NOT going to let her get to Garrett again.

"Now, I don't see your little cousin who catches fireballs around. Can you do the same thing?"

Charlotte glared at her but did not answer.

"No? So, you can't fight fire with fire?"

Charlotte suddenly broke into a huge grin.

"That's exactly what I'm going to do, old woman."

As Hexa's face wrinkled into anger, Charlotte mumbled a few words, blinked, and turned herself into a forty foot dragon. She had read a book about a dragon to Garrett when he was small, and she now matched the drawings of the dragon as best as she could remember. She was dark green with thick scales. She had a long, think tail, a large head with bright yellow eyes and black horns. She imagined she looked fierce. She added to the look now with a deep, rumbling growl.

The witch stepped backward, surprised at the remarkable transformation, but quickly recovered. She tried to snatch the initiative by reaching back and throwing a fireball at Charlotte, but it just bounced off Charlotte's now very thick skin.

My turn, Charlotte thought to herself. She took a deep breath and blew it out at the witch, expecting a withering stream of flame, but nothing happened. Hexa grinned an evil grin.

"That's it? No fire inside of you? Or did you just forget how to light it up?"

Charlotte frantically tried to figure out how to breathe fire. She suddenly remembered a children's story Nana had read to her years ago about how dragons breathed fire. According to the children's story, they ate grass and swallowed crystals. The grass created gas and the crystals were rubbed together inside the dragons throat to light the gas, and voila! The dragon breathed fire.

With nothing else to go on, Charlotte quickly ripped up as much grass as she could, chewed it and swallowed. She frantically looked around, knowing she would not find any crystals, but trying to figure out what else she could use to light the gas.

Hexa was trying to get around her to look for Garrett, so she kept moving back and forth, which helped her generate gas, but how to light it? Hexa moved to Charlotte's left and Charlotte lashed out with her tail and crashed it into a car, almost overturning it.

Suddenly Charlotte remembered working with her friends in robotics, building a remote controlled robot. The battery they used for power was a rectangular affair that the boys would play with, getting a spark from it by holding a screw driver against one pole and touching it to the other pole.

Charlotte reached out with her front legs and tore the hood off of the car she had just dented with her tail. She found the battery and ripped it out of the engine compartment and stuffed it into her mouth, along with a piece of metal from the battery support. She turned back toward the witch, who had watched the process.

"So, now you're going to eat a car?" cackled the witch. "Is that supposed to impress me?"

Charlotte felt a huge burp coming and shifted the battery and the piece of metal she had eaten around in her mouth in preparation. When the burp came, she touched the metal rod to the two ends of the battery and released the burp.

The spark from touching the battery poles together ignited the gas and a huge flame shot out of her mouth like a giant blow torch. She aimed it at the witch and held it there for a full three seconds until the burp ended. When the flame stopped, she peered down, waiting for the smoke to clear. All that was left was smoldering cement, scorched dirt on all sides, and a badly scarred car. Hexa was gone.

Charlotte checked in all directions, but didn't see her anywhere. She spit out the battery and metal and changed back to her normal self, then looked around for Garrett.

"Buddy, it's OK," she called out. "You can change back. She's gone." Garrett suddenly appeared from behind a tree.

"Are you OK?" she asked him. He nodded and then smiled.

"That was awesome, Charlotte. When we get to school, can you do that for my friends?"

"No, I don't think that's such a good idea."

She looked around and saw several doors opening in the neighborhood and women stepping out. The ground was still smoking and the car was now not only dented and without a hood, but charred black. She thought they'd better get out of there before anyone began to ask questions. She took Garrett's hand.

"Let's go home for now. I'm a little too tired to go to school today."

"Really?" Garrett replied, the obvious glee showing in his voice.

"Yeah. I'll call mom and tell her there was a fire on the street on our way to school and we'd rather stay at home for now."

"OK. Can we go to CC's so I can play video games and watch movies?"

"All day, if you want," she said, nervously looking around at the growing crowd. She definitely didn't want to hang around and have to answer any questions about what might have just happened.

"Awesome. Let's go," Garrett said.

They turned around and Charlotte quickly guided him away from the still smoking scene toward the safety of home.

CHAPTER SEVENTY ONE

They all met at CC's that afternoon and Charlotte described her encounter with Hexa to the group.

"You actually turned into a dragon?" Annabelle asked, somewhat disgusted with the idea.

"It was the only think I could think of," replied Charlotte and the group all nodded.

"It was way cool," Garrett chimed in and they all laughed.

"I'm surprised. I thought you could only turn into real animals," Henry offered.

"Me too. But I couldn't think of a real one that could stand up to the witch. Then I." Charlotte paused and looked at the flat screen. When she continued it was almost a whisper. "Then, when Hexa said something about fighting fire with fire, I thought of a dragon, and I wished I could turn into one, even though it wasn't part of my original wish. And something, or someone, sort of told me I should try it."

The flat screen showed soft, gentle colors and Charlotte nodded her understanding. CC had granted her wish.

"So, maybe with me throwing the fireballs back at her and you being a dragon, we can beat her," Quinn suddenly interjected. The flat screen suddenly burst into action, dark colors swirling angrily.

"Ok, OK. So, maybe not," Quinn said in response to CC's anger.

"Let's focus here," Henry jumped in. "Did everyone bring their triangles?"

Everyone nodded except Garrett.

"Not me," he said, very quietly.

"Why not?" asked Chugga, and Charlotte stepped in to answer for Garrett.

"He hasn't found one yet."

"Maybe we don't need one from Garrett. We have five, right?" Annabelle reasoned. "And that's how many points there are on a star."

"Let's see," said Henry.

Everyone moved to the table that had appeared in front of the flat screen. Inscribed on the table was an outline of a star with indications as to where the five triangles should be placed. A letter appeared inside each drawn triangle. Everyone placed their triangles in the marked area that had their initial on it, creating a perfect star.

"Now what?" asked Chugga as they all stared at the shape. Nothing happened for a moment, then the table began to glow a soft green. The color slowly shrank away until it was only showing in the hexagon in the center of the five pointed star.

"We're missing the piece in the middle," Chugga said.

"I have one of those!" Garrett blurted out. "I found it lying on the floor when we were all coming out of the building the day you got me away from the witch."

"Awesome, Buddy," Henry said. "Where is it? Is it in your room? Can you go get it?"

Garrett shook his head.

"It's in my desk at school. I took it there to show my friends."

Everyone else sagged. It was Friday afternoon. They'd have to wait until Monday to complete the star. Disappointed, they all headed for home.

CHAPTER SEVENTY TWO

It was Saturday evening and Annabelle was out in the open field, gathering the horses to bring them into the stables for the night. She was walking alongside Beau, and they were chatting about the day when a shadow crossed their path. Beau immediately stopped walking and Annabelle looked up to see Hexa. She sucked in a quick breath. It was her turn to face the witch.

"Good evening, young lady," Hexa said in a scratchy voice. "I thought I'd stop by and invite you to come visit me. I believe I've found a much better hiding place than the one your cousins and your meddling Grandfather were able to find. I hope you'll come along quietly."

Beau suddenly reared up and pawed the air right in front of Hexa, but she didn't seem disturbed. Instead she waved a wand and Beau froze in midair. Hexa stepped around him and looked at Annabelle.

"Shall we go now?"

Annabelle looked at Beau, who was still suspended in the air standing on his hind legs like a statue. Annabelle could see his eyes moving, and she saw both fear and anger in them.

"Let him go," she almost shouted at Hexa.

"Oh, he'll be fine."

"Let him go right now," Annabelle ordered, and Hexa nodded.

"All right. I think he's learned his lesson."

She waved her hand again and Beau's front legs dropped to the ground. He glared at Hexa, then turned and bolted back into the field. Hexa watched him go and then turned back to Annabelle.

"Seems like your friend is a coward."

"He is not," Annabelle said crossly. But she did feel disappointed that Beau had deserted her. Hexa held out her hand.

"Give me your hand. We'll use magic this time. Human travel machines are too slow, and too easy to follow."

Annabelle took a step backward and Hexa shook her head.

"You might as well come along, dear. I know your power is the ability to talk to animals. I heard you in the barn that first day. That power won't help you at all now."

Annabelle took another step backward and suddenly heard a low thunder starting to roll in the distance. She glanced up but didn't see any dark clouds and wondered if the sound had something to do with Hexa's travel plans. But then Hexa heard it too. The sound was coming from the field and it was growing.

They both turned and faced the field and Annabelle's heart soared. Beau hadn't run away in fear. He had gone to get help! Annabelle almost grinned as she saw nine horses thundering toward them. She glanced at Hexa and saw concern on her face. Maybe she didn't have enough power to stop all nine of them like she had done with Beau.

But then Hexa raised her hand and made a swirling motion. Annabelle looked back at the field and was shocked to see the ground in front of the horses ripped up and thrown into the air. For a moment she couldn't see them at all, but then they burst through the clutter that was still hanging in the air and thundered on toward them.

Hexa waved her other hand and lightning bolts slashed out of the sky and crashed into the ground in front of the horses. They shied at first, but Beau seemed to rally them and they continued on. They were now close enough that Annabelle could see their eyes, and she could see the determination in them. They were going to save her or die trying.

Annabelle slowly moved away from Hexa while she was focused on the horses. She didn't want to be standing close to her when the horses arrived if she could help it. She glanced back at the witch and she could see her frustration. She wondered why the witch hadn't shot the lightning bolts directly at the horses instead of right in front of them. Maybe she didn't have the power to actually kill something!

Hexa shuddered in frustration.

"Your little parlor trick of talking to the animals seems to have made them fond of you." She glanced at the horses, now only yards away and still charging, intent on running down the witch.

"You haven't seen the last of me," Hexa snarled and disappeared. The horses seemed surprised at first, but quickly recovered and stopped right in front of Annabelle. She hugged Beau first, then all of the others in succession.

"Thank you. All of you," she murmured as she made the rounds. When their breathing had returned to normal,

Annabelle and the nine horses slowly walked to the barn, chattering all the way about their exciting experience.

CHAPTER SEVENTY THREE

It seemed to the cousins that the week end was the longest one ever. Finally Monday came and dragged on for what seemed like days before they could finally get home from school and meet at CC's. Charlotte had insured that Garrett brought home the center piece and had taken it with him when he went into his closet.

Everyone gathered around him now as he produced the coveted piece, and watched as he placed it into the open space between the bases of the five triangles. It fit perfectly and the flat screen came to life with dancing colors. They all glanced up at the screen, enjoying the light show.

Suddenly Quinn shouted.

"Hey, look at this."

Everyone turned around and saw the newly formed star slowly lifting off the table and floating about a foot above it. When Quinn reached for out it, the star danced away, just out of reach. Chugga laughed and tried to grab it himself, but it moved away from him too.

"What's going on?" Quinn asked.

"It's a star made by all of us, so maybe we all have to reach for it at the same time," suggested Charlotte.

"Let's try it," Quinn said and they surrounded the table and looked at Henry.

"OK, on the count of three, we do it," Henry said.

They all nodded and Henry counted it down.

"One, two."

"Wait!" Garrett said. "You can all grab points of the star, but what do I grab?"

They looked at Charlotte for an answer, since she had thought of the idea of all of them reaching for it at the same time. Charlotte thought for a moment, playing different approaches out in her mind.

"Well, maybe we all touch a point on the star and bring it to you and you touch the center."

"OK." Garrett said and they all readied again.

"I'll start over," Henry said. "On three. One, two, three."

They all reached toward the star and it floated steadily as they all five touched a different point on the star and collectively pulled it toward Garrett. He reached out and touched the middle of the star and it burst into brilliant colors and shot away from them, floating above their heads near the ceiling.

"Well," Chugga said. "I guess that went well."

"Now what?" Quinn said, articulating what everyone else was wondering. As they watched, the star slowly drifted toward the table and settled back onto its original layout, but it still maintained its brilliant color.

"Look," Chugga said. "The table's changed shape," Chugga said, pointing toward the table. They all looked and Quinn agreed.

"Yeah. It's, like, six sided," he said.

"A hexagon," Annabelle said and Quinn just smiled.

"That's appropriate," he said.

Suddenly colored lines appeared on the table, one from the tip of each of the star points and one from the center of the star. At the point where the lines met the end the table, a letter appeared.

"Look," Chugga said. "The letters are back."

"One for each of us," Quinn pointed out and sat down in the chair facing the red line with the letter Q at the base. Everyone else took their places around the table at their designated spots and waited. Nothing happened for a few minutes and Garrett began to get restless.

"Charlotte, can I go to my room and watch a movie?"

"Not right now, buddy. Let's see what's going to happen next."

Garrett sighed, not really interested in the lines on the table. But finally, the flat screen came to life and the colors on the screen swirled and morphed into a portrait of Hexa.

"Now we're getting somewhere," Quinn quipped and Henry broke in.

"I think it's time for us to figure out how to defeat Hexa. I think the star will help us."

"How?" asked Chugga and Annabelle offered her opinion.

"Maybe it will make us smarter, or help us with clues, or something."

"So, we're supposed to, like, guess how to defeat her?" Chugga asked.

"I don't know." Henry replied. "Let's just talk about it and see what happens."

"Fine," Quinn said. "But I'm not very good at talking about things."

Charlotte just smiled.

"That's OK. There are two girls here. More than enough to carry the conversation."

"Tell me about it," Chugga said and slumped down into his seat, preparing for a long, boring conversation. Little did he know he was in for a big surprise.

CHAPTER SEVENTY FOUR

Charlotte took the lead and began by restating their problem.

"So, what we need to determine is, how do we vanquish Hexa, the witch, so she won't be constantly threatening us and endeavoring to get into CC's. Does that summarize the situation?"

She looked around the room and Annabelle and Henry nodded their agreement, while the other boys just looked at her. Finally Chugga spoke.

"English, Charlotte."

She smiled.

"We want to get rid of Hexa, for good."

Chugga's face brightened.

"See, I knew you could do it!"

"I still don't see why we can't kill her," Quinn said.

"Grandpa said he didn't think we could kill her. He doesn't think she can die," Henry reminded Quinn.

"But everybody dies," Chugga said.

"Every human, but not necessarily witches," Annabelle said.

"Can we scare her away?" asked Garrett.

Chugga shook his head.

"She hasn't left so far, and we've done about everything we can possibly do to her with the powers we have."

Suddenly the flat screen jumped to life and they all looked at it, waiting. It swirled its dark colors, indicating the statement was not true.

"What powers do we have that we haven't used yet?" Quinn asked, and the star on the table began to pulse bright green.

"Oh!" Annabelle said. "Our new star must have special powers."

"So maybe we can use it against the witch," Quinn said.

"How?" asked Garrett. "It's not very big, and it doesn't look like it could hurt someone."

"But maybe it has a special magic we can use," suggested Chugga.

"Like what?" asked Quinn.

They all stared at the star, still pulsing on the table. What could its power be?

"We'll never guess what power it has," Quinn said.

"Maybe we can wish that we knew the star's power," offered Henry.

Annabelle shook her head.

"Something tells me that won't work. I think maybe we should go back to the original question. What can we do to get rid of Hexa? If we can answer that, I think the star will have the power to help us do whatever that is."

The flat screen swirled in agreement, so Henry decided to get them started.

"Let's think about our meetings with the witch so far. What have we said or done that seemed to bother her?"

"She was really mad that I could catch her fireballs and send them back," Quinn started.

"And she seemed afraid of the hoses when they were all trying to run her down," Annabelle added.

"And she disappeared when I breathed fire at her as a dragon," said Charlotte.

They all went quiet, pondering the problem.

"All of those are true, but we can't always plan on having a bunch of horses around, or Charlotte to turn into a dragon, or Quinn to play catch with her," Henry said. "We need something that will last."

They kicked the problem around for another fifteen minutes and got nowhere. Finally Garrett piped up.

"Why don't we ask Grandpa? I bet he'll know what to do."

"Great idea," Henry said. He closed his eyes and tried to teleconnect with Grandpa.

"Hey, Grandpa. It's Henry. We need to talk to you."

There was no answer.

"That's weird," Henry said and tried again.

"Grandpa, can you hear me?"

Again there was no answer. Then Chugga remembered.

"Wait. Aren't Grandpa with Nana in Germany on vacation?"

Henry slumped.

"Oh, yeah. You're right."

"But I didn't think there was a limit to teleconnecting. I thought it would work all over the world." Henry complained.

"Maybe he turned it off," Garrett suggested.

Quinn snorted. "You can't turn it off."

"Yes, you can. The witch turned mine off when I was in that room," Garrett replied.

Everyone nodded.

"But they get back tomorrow, I think," Annabelle said.

"OK. Let's try to get ahold of Grandpa tomorrow and meet here again as soon as he can," Henry said, ending the meeting. Everyone got up from the table and went to their own rooms, then headed home.

CHAPTER SEVENTY FIVE

Grandpa and Nana landed the next day and were on their way home in an Uber car when Henry teleconnected.

"Grandpa, are you home yet?"

Grandpa answered almost immediately.

"Hey, Henry. We're in a car coming from the airport. What's up?"

Henry let out a sigh of relief.

"We've been trying to get in touch with you, but it hasn't worked."

"Really?"

"Yeah. Garrett thought maybe the witch had turned off your teleconnecting power."

"I doubt that she could do that."

"He said she blocked him when she kidnapped him."

"Maybe up close she could do something like that, but I don't think she's strong enough to block me from a distance."

"Anyway, we're glad you're back. We need your help."

"With Hexa?"

"Yeah."

"Henry, I already told you I couldn't help you defeat her."

"We know, but we're hoping you can at least give us some ideas on what we can do to beat her."

"OK. I can do that, I guess."

"Great. Any chance you can meet us at CC's tonight?"

"I'm pretty tired right now from the trip. How about tomorrow?"

Henry sighed again. Another day lost!

"Well, OK, I guess."

"Great. When?"

"Around four in the afternoon?"

"I'll be there."

"Thanks, Grandpa. Say hi to Nana for me."

"Sure."

"Bye."

Henry shook his head. Better late than never, he thought to himself and began teleconnecting the group to tell them about the meeting.

CHAPTER SEVENTY SIX

The next day Grandpa was already at CC's when the cousins started arriving. They found him in the living room watching a movie on the big flat screen, eating popcorn and sipping a Coke.

"Hey, Grandpa!" Quinn said when he came through his door. Grandpa smiled and waved.

"Hey, Quinn. How've you been?"

"Good."

"How's Lacrosse going?"

"Great."

Charlotte and Garrett entered next and both of them ran up to Grandpa for hugs, and within a few more minutes the group was complete. When everyone was finished collecting their favorite snacks from the food table, Grandpa looked at them all and smiled.

"So, it made me feel pretty good that you guys were in such a hurry to see me. Must be my winning personality, right?"

"Must be," Chugga said with a smile.

"OK. Let's get serious, what's up?"

Henry took the lead.

"Hexa has tried her intimidation stuff again. She tried to grab Charlotte and Garrett on their way to school one day, and then she tried to get Annabelle when she was bringing in the horses one evening."

"What happened?"

"You're going to love this," Chugga said. "Charlotte turned into a dragon and toasted Hexa."

Grandpa's eyes got big as he looked at Charlotte.

"You can turn into a dragon? That is so cool!"

"I know, right?" Charlotte said with pride. Grandpa held up his hand and Charlotte high fived him. Then he looked at Annabelle.

"How did you deal with her?"

"Well, I was conversing with Beau when she just popped up out of nowhere. He tried to kick her but she, like, froze him."

"Really?"

"Yes. But then she let him go and he ran away, but not to hide. He ran to get the other horses and they came back together and scared her away."

"Awesome."

"But we can't keep doing this forever. We need to deal with her," Henry cut in.

"CC gave us this really cool star," Chugga said. "And we think it's magic. But we don't know how to use it."

"So we're trying to figure out what Hexa is afraid of," Quinn added. "And we thought maybe you could help us figure that out."

"Hmm," Grandpa said, still munching popcorn while they spoke. "Let's see," he said and then paused, thinking.

"Well, she used to hate water, but my bet is she's cured herself of that." He paused and they all waited. "But, when she was here before, the clubhouse was fighting her by putting up a wall of ice. And the clubhouse must know something, right? And, when I used 'me too' to push her into the ice wall, she screamed and thrashed around and finally disappeared."

"So, maybe ice is the answer," Chugga said and the flat screen, which had gone dark when they started their conversation, burst into bright colors and swirled happily around. Grandpa was startled.

"What the heck is that?" he asked.

"Oh, that's how CC talks to us," Quinn said.

"You talk to the clubhouse?" Grandpa asked, wrinkling his brow.

"Yeah. Pretty cool, huh?" Quinn replied.

"Amazing," Grandpa said, shaking his head. "What does that mean?" he asked pointing at the image on the flat screen.

"It means we got it right. Freezing is how we can get rid of Hexa," Chugga said, very excited.

"Now the question is, how do we do it?" Charlotte said.

"I have no idea," Chugga said as he tried to figure out how the small star would work. They all looked at Grandpa and he just shrugged.

"Well, you don't need me here anymore," he said and got up and walked over to the door to his room. He stopped and turned back toward them.

"You're all very smart kids. You'll figure it out," he said and went through his door, still munching on his popcorn.

CHAPTER SEVENTY SEVEN

They all watched in disbelief as Grandpa disappeared into his room. A few seconds after the door to his room closed, it disappeared, indicating he had gone into the closet and then home, leaving his room empty.

"Well, that wasn't what I'd hoped for," Quinn quipped.

"Yeah," Chugga said. "We still don't know how to use the star."

"I think Grandpa is positive that we have to do this ourselves in order for it to work properly" Annabelle said.

As she said it, the star began to glow again and slowly lifted up from the table. It separated into its six pieces and they floated around for a moment before reforming into a shiny silver box. Then, the box moved off to the side of the room and settled onto the floor where it slowly began to grow larger and larger until it was about six feet on each side.

"Awesome," Quinn said.

"Now it's big enough to put Hexa inside," declared Charlotte.

"Even with her pointy hat on," Garrett agreed with a grim, determined look.

As they continued to stare at the box, the sides of it turned icy. The box was now so cold it was cooling the entire room.

"It's a giant refrigerator," Chugga said. "Grandpa said he thought that Hexa might be afraid of ice and CC agreed. This is it!"

"But how do we get her inside it?" asked Quinn with a frown.

"Maybe each one of us takes one of the six sides and then we close it around her," suggested Annabelle with a shrug.

"But I can't lift my side," Garrett protested, studying the box.

"I don't think any of us can lift a side," Henry agreed.

"Maybe we build most of the box and somehow lure Hexa into it, and then close the rest of it on her," Quinn said.

"OK. That sounds like a good idea. Now we just have to figure out how to get it done," Henry said, and they all settled down to work out a plan.

CHAPTER SEVENTY EIGHT

Three days later, Chugga was walking through his home town of Wayne on his way home from middle school with a few friends when they decided to make a brief stop at the Dunkin' Donuts store for a quick snack. After buying and eating their snacks, and checking out the girls who were giggling in the corner, the trio of boys left the store. As they did, they split up, each going his separate direction toward home.

Chugga was walking alone, carefully looking around as he went. He was a block away from the turn onto the street he lived on when a shadow passed across his path and he felt a sudden chill. He stopped and looked around, but didn't see anything, so he continued walking. Everything was fine until he turned the corner onto his street and he was confronted by a dark figure blocking his path. He stopped and instinctively took a few steps back.

"Well, hello. It's Weston, isn't it?" Hexa wheezed as she peered at him.

"Everyone calls me Chugga," he said softly, still backing up a little as he spoke.

"Ah, yes. Chugga. And how are you today?"

"I was fine until you showed up," Chugga replied, trying his best to be brave. He knew he could always time travel if things got really bad with Hexa, but still....

"Need a lift?" Hexa croaked and then cackled a harsh laugh.

"Why, you got your broom with you?" Chugga retorted, still trying to be brave. Hexa just waved a hand at him.

"Old fashioned. I have much more modern methods of travel. Care to see?"

Chugga shook his head and glanced around, hoping to see someone else on the street, but it was bare. He was definitely alone.

"I just want to go home," he said.

"Of course. And I just want to get inside your clubhouse. Maybe we can make a deal."

"What kind of a deal do you have in mind?" Chugga said cautiously.

"I'll let you go home, completely unharmed, right now, and you meet me later at your clubhouse and let me in." She peered at him, her green eyes flashing, and then she continued. "Unless, of course, you have some sort of super power that you think will save you from me. A few of your cousins have been very lucky in that department recently."

Chugga shook his head.

"No. My super power isn't going to help me," he said with a sad shrug. "So, I guess it's best if I just do what you ask."

Hexa was surprised and studied his face for a long moment before answering.

"I think you're agreeing awfully quickly, young man."

Chugga shrugged.

"I can use my super power and get away from you, but it won't make you go away or give up. I don't think you'll ever give up. My cousins want to keep fighting you, but I think it's a waste of time. I think we might as well give you what you want now so you'll let us alone."

"Well, a sensible young man. Good for you," she said enthusiastically. "When should I meet you at the club house?"

Chugga thought about it for a moment before answering.

"Not today. There will be others there today."

"All right. When?"

"Tomorrow. Everyone has plans for tomorrow after school, so no one will be at the clubhouse until after dinner. So, I guess I could meet you there at, say around four o'clock?"

"None of the others will be there? Not the fire thrower or the dragon?"

Chugga shook his head. "No, they'll all be in after school programs tomorrow. Henry has," he continued but she waved him off.

"Never mind. I don't care what they're into, as long as they won't be there."

Hexa studied him for another moment before agreeing to the time.

"Excellent. Four o'clock then."

"OK."

"Don't be late. And, don't try to double cross me. Believe me, I can make things very uncomfortable for you."

"Don't worry. I just want this all to be over," Chugga said.

"Done," Hexa said and waved a hand in the air. There was a blindingly bright flash of light, and when Chugga could see again, she was gone.

CHAPTER SEVENTY NINE

Chugga was nervous. At least he liked to think he was nervous, rather than scared. He was standing out in front of CC's, all alone and very vulnerable. He had arrived early because he didn't want Hexa to be right at the front door when he stepped out. He wanted the door closed behind him, giving him at least a little leverage.

He looked around the clearing again, studying everything, wondering if Hexa was already out there, watching him. He glanced at his watch, more for the self-assurance that he could time travel away from Hexa if things got really bad, than to check the time.

3:55

It was still a little early, but there was suddenly a rustle among the trees a little to the right. His stomach tightened when he saw Hexa appear and come gliding toward him. And she really was gliding, not walking. He wondered how she did that, which helped him ignore the knot that had formed in his stomach and seemed to be growing.

What was he doing here? What if she became incensed by something he said or did? Could he time travel fast enough to avoid whatever terrible retaliation she could throw at him? He certainly couldn't deal with her fireballs like Quinn could. Or fight fire with fire like Charlotte had. This was a bad idea, he thought to himself. A very bad idea.

Hexa's gliding shape came to a halt a few feet in front of him and she peered at him intently with her scary green eyes.

"So, you are going to keep your end of the bargain. I thought you'd try to renege."

"Like I said yesterday," Chugga said. "I just want this to be over.

Hexa nodded and slowly looked around, sniffing the air.

"And you're here alone? I don't want to play catch with that brother of yours again." She shook her head. "Such a waste of time in the overall scheme of things, don't you think?"

Chugga nodded.

"Why do you want to get into the clubhouse anyway?"

"It was mine once, a long time ago. I found it and I made it mine. It has special powers and it gave some to me."

"So, what happened?"

Hexa's face clouded over.

"Your great, great grandfather came along. He was lumberjacking, and found the caboose where it was hidden in the woods. He wanted to come in and, like a fool, I let him. He asked for some silly powers, something about being a mechanical wizard, and his friends were impressed."

"Why was that bad?" Chugga asked.

"Because he wanted to let all of his friends in. He was persistent and I had to use some strong persuasions on his friends to keep them out."

"Then what happened?"

"I went out one day and when I came back, the clubhouse was gone. He stole it from me."

"Maybe he didn't do it. Maybe the clubhouse left because you were doing bad things with your powers."

Hexa's green eyes suddenly flashed and Chugga winced in pain. He'd pushed too hard and now he regretted it.

"I'll not have you judging me, boy. I did what I thought I had to do to protect what was mine, and he still took it away from me."

"And now you found it and want it back," Chugga said.

Hexa looked longingly at the clubhouse behind Chugga.

"Its power seems to have grown immensely. Imagine the things I could do if I could harness that power now."

Chugga glanced over his shoulder at CC. The front wall was closed solid and was thick with ice. CC definitely did not want to let Hexa inside. He took a deep breath, preparing for the next step.

"Well, let's get this over with," he said and turned toward the clubhouse.

"CC. Let us come inside," he said loudly. At first nothing happened, so he said it again.

"CC, let us in, right now."

He stood between CC and Hexa and watched as the wall slowly began to melt. CC was letting down its defenses. He took a deep breath. He knew that one way or another, the end was near.

CHAPTER EIGHTY

Hexa's eyes grew greedy as she watched the front wall of the club house slowly receding and gradually warming. She had trouble controlling her excitement.

"You have chosen wisely, you know," she almost whispered to Chugga. "Your cousins will see it too. Once I have control of this marvelous structure, I will leave you all alone, and your lives can go back to their dreary, normal ways."

Chugga nodded and glanced nervously at the edges of the clearing.

"That's good," he managed to mumble in response.

With her goal so close, Hexa was getting impatient.

"What's taking so long?" She muttered as she stepped closer to the wall. But it was still too cold for her, and she had to step back again. She glared at Chugga as if the slow movement was his fault, but he just shrugged.

"Maybe it doesn't really want to open up. Maybe that's why it's going so slowly," he argued, speaking with a sad face.

"Well, if it doesn't start moving faster, it will definitely pay once I get control of it again," Hexa threatened.

The wall continued at its own pace, and finally it had returned to its normal dimensions. Hexa rubbed her hands together in anticipation, small sparks flying from them as if her hands were made of flint. Chugga was alarmed at the sight, but it turned out to be harmless. They waited as the door reappeared in the wall. Chugga stepped out of the way and Hexa took a step toward the door and then stopped. She leaned forward and pushed the door open, then peered into the inside of the caboose. She turned back to Chugga.

"Why is it so dark in there? I can't see a thing," she complained.

"I don't know. Maybe the lights don't go on until somebody goes inside," he replied.

"You don't know?" she said.

Chugga shook his head.

"I guess I've never been the first one to go into it."

Hexa studied his face. Suddenly she spun around and stared out at the clearing, searching the trees around it.

"What's the matter?" Chugga asked.

"I thought I sensed something, or someone," Hexa said, then shrugged. "Maybe not."

She turned back to Chugga

"Why don't you go in first?" she suggested as she continued to try to read him. He stared back at her and shrugged.

"I thought you were so anxious to get in," he said to her.

"I am. But I am also a cautious person," she replied. She held her hand out toward the door.

"After you, young man."

Chugga glanced at the open door inviting them in and hesitated.

"Are you sure?"

"Oh, I insist."

Chugga shrugged.

"OK, I'll go first," he said firmly. He stepped up on the small landing, paused for a moment, and then stepped into the dark.

CHAPTER EIGHTY ONE

Chugga stepped cautiously through the open door and kept walking slowly ahead through the darkness. When he had taken three steps, he stopped and turned around.

"OK, I'm in," he called out and Hexa immediately responded.

"Turn on the lights. I want to see what's inside," she called back.

"I can't find the switch in the dark," Chugga called back out to her.

Her impatience finally overcame her caution and Hexa stepped up to the door. But again she paused and turned around, scanning the edges of the clearing. There was something nagging at the back of her consciousness, and she couldn't make it go away. When she didn't see anything, she turned back to the door and stepped inside.

It was just as dark as it had appeared from the outside. She paused, waiting for her eyes to grow accustomed to the dark. When they didn't, she held up a hand, waved it in a small circle and a torch appeared. It lit the area directly around her but its light seemed to quickly get lost as it moved away from her. She could only see a foot or so in front of her, but it was enough for her to keep going if she dared. She paused again to consider her options.

Finally she realized this was probably the clubhouse fighting her, so she took another step and then another. On the next step she bumped into a wall, and suddenly all of her warning senses exploded. She whirled around caught a glimpse of a young boy smiling at her. Her brain processed the image and decided it was the boy who had caught her fireballs and threw them back at her. She raised her hand to fire a lightning bolt at him and suddenly the sight disappeared, and her world turned completely black. And then it began to get cold. Very cold.

CHAPTER EIGHTY TWO

They had planned it for days. They had decided that Chugga would be the bait, as he was one of the few of them who Hexa had not yet tried to force into letting her into the clubhouse. He had walked home alone from school for three days before she finally showed up. And the plan had worked perfectly.

At first they had not been able to figure out how to use the box they could construct out of the special star. When the six sides grew to a size large enough to trap the witch inside, they were too heavy for them to move at all. All six of them together couldn't lift even one side off the floor, much less move it in front of the door and then put all of the other pieces together into a box.

And then Garrett had solved the problem by saying out loud "I wish we could use magic to move the walls of the box."

Suddenly the sides became almost weightless and they easily built five sides of the box just inside the front door, making a floor, two sides, the top and the back. Then came the problem of securing the final side of the box once Hexa was lured inside, assuming that was possible. Surely she could stop it from happening if she saw it coming.

Finally Annabelle suggested that the last piece could be hidden out in the woods, and Quinn could teleport it into place when he knew Hexa was inside the rest of the box. After that, it was a matter of everyone staying out of sight until Chugga was able to lure the witch into position. When she was finally there and Chugga had slipped out the back of the box, Quinn moved the last piece right outside the front door. He was supposed to teleport it directly into place, but he couldn't resist the temptation to have Hexa see who it was that was sealing her fate.

Fortunately for all of them, he was quick enough to show his face to Hexa and still teleport the final side into place before she could react. Once the box was complete with Hexa safely inside, it sealed itself tight and began the cooling process.

They were all standing around the box now, celebrating.

"This is so cool," Quinn said, a huge smile on his face.

"No pun intended," Annabelle said with a small smile of her own.

"You were so awesome, Chugga," Charlotte said. "I'm so proud."

"Yeah, you really tricked her," Henry added as he slapped Chugga on the back.

"Were you scared?" Garrett asked, peering up at Chugga.

"Nah," Chugga said, but when Quinn raised his eyebrows at him he recanted. "Well, a little bit, sometimes, maybe."

They all had Cokes or lemonade and were toasting themselves and CC over and over again. When they finally calmed down, Garrett asked another question.

"Are we safe now? Will she stay in there forever?"

Charlotte looked around at the group before she answered.

"Good question, buddy. Anybody have any ideas about that?"

Henry answered first.

"I think so. I don't think CC would have come up with a plan that only kept her out of our hair for a little while."

"So, what are we supposed to do with the box now?" asked Quinn. "We can't just leave it here next to the food table forever."

"Yeah. The farther away we can send it, the better," said Chugga.

"Send it? You mean, like Fed Ex or something?" asked Charlotte.

"I don't know. I was thinking maybe Quinn could teleport it somewhere that would be safe."

They all looked at Quinn.

"Do you think you could teleport it?" Annabelle asked.

Quinn shrugged.

"Sure. Why not?"

"The question is, where to send it?" Henry asked, looking at the group. "Any ideas?"

They were all quiet for a long time before Chugga finally broke into a big smile.

"I have an idea," he said and leaned toward Quinn and whispered a suggestion.

Quinn nodded.

"I could try that. Why not?" he said and walked over to the box. He stood next to it for a long time with his eyes closed. He finally opened them and put both hands on the box then pulled them back quickly.

"Wow, it's really cold," he said with a smile. "I'll have to do this fast."

He focused again for a moment, then reached out and touched the box. He blinked and the box disappeared.

CHAPTER EIGHTY THREE

All three Gallahan boys were sitting on the couch in their living room watching the news with their parents. Dinner had been good and they were stalling before having to go do homework, and watching the news was as good an excuse as any to keep from getting sent upstairs. The announcer was working his way through the top news stories and was down to item number six.

"Scientists today reported a powerful impact as a meteor struck the moon. This is not all that unusual, but normally scientists track asteroids that come close to the earth or the moon. Today's impact was unusual in that there were no asteroids being tracked. Scientists can't explain where the asteroid came from, and are reviewing previous data."

The screen changed to a man with wild hair and glasses with a name and a long title under his face.

"The object that impacted the moon just appeared out of nowhere. One minute it wasn't there, and the next it crashed into the surface of the moon. Very strange."

The screen changed back to the lead news announcer.

"The weather is up next, right after these messages."

Henry and Chugga looked at Quinn, who had a quiet smile playing at the corners of his mouth. He looked over at Chugga, who reached out his hand. They fist bumped just as their mother spoke.

"OK. No more stalling. Time for homework. If you study really hard, maybe someday one of you will be a scientist like the guy on TV. Maybe you can figure out what happened on the moon today."

Henry leaned toward his two brothers and whispered "Hexa arrived!", and they all stood and trudged up to their rooms.